i

TYE WATKINS
IN

Desperate Trail

Book IV of the Tye Watkins Series

BY
GARY MCMILLAN

Cover Concept and Design by Michael McMillan

Authors' Discovery Cooperation, Inc.
165 Cherry Lane
Robert Lee, Texas 79764
325-453-4595

Published by: Authors' Discovery Cooperation, Inc. September 2008

ISBN Number   978-0-9800854-3-3

Printed in the United States of America

BOOKS IN THE TYE WATKINS SERIES

BORDER TROUBLE
THE CROSSING
YANCEY

Dedication

To my mother-in-law, Carolyn Emerson, who has been in the hospital for several weeks. I would like to thank my good friend Garry Garner, my Brother-in-law, Ronnie Humphries, and Emma Dudney for their critiquing of "The Desperate Trail".

Author's Note

At the outbreak of the Civil War, all the federal troops were removed from the forts in Texas and shipped back east to fight the Confederacy. The State was left unprotected from the Apache, Comanche, and the notorious bandit gangs that now roamed the area unmolested. No place was more dangerous during this period of time than along the Texas/Mexico Border where you had the Apache and the bandit gangs jumping back and forth across the Border.

After the War, the old forts were regarrisoned in Texas and several new forts were established. This was a plan to form a line of defense against the raiding Indians and the bandits. Fort Clark was regarrisoned in 1866. Due to its close proximity to the Border, the fort was expected to patrol almost a hundred miles of the Rio Grande River which separated Texas and Mexico.

The history of Fort Clark was filled with clashes with the Apache, occasionally with the Comanche, and always with the bandit gangs that crossed freely back and forth across the Border, preying on the homesteaders.

The Tye Watkins Series of books attempt to portray this danger. The stories center on Tye, who is Chief of Scouts at Clark in 1868. He is continually putting himself at risk trying to protect the homesteaders living in the area as well as keeping the troops he scouts for out of harms way.

~~~

Ben Watkins was a well known mountain man back in the days of the beaver craze from the early 1800's to 1836. When the demand for beaver ended, he moved to Texas where he met Lori. They were married and built a small homestead near the Texas/Mexico border. They had a son, Tye, who was born in 1839.

Ben, being an old mountain man, was an expert in all aspects of survival: tracking, reading sign, hunting, knife fighting Indian style, wrestling, shooting, and bare knuckle fighting. He began to teach young Tye these things almost from the time the youngster could walk. Ben was killed while with the Rangers when Tye was seventeen. Since that time, Tye has honed all the skills and lessons Ben had taught him to where he was now one of the best known scouts in Texas. He was feared by the bandits and respected as a great warrior by the Apache.

DESPERATE TRAIL

Three weeks earlier, Tye had brought in the most vicious outlaw he had ever encountered, Yancey Cates. Yancey, along with his brother and other ex-Confederate soldiers who had come to the area resented the Union and anything that represented Unionist authority. During a robbery, they killed some soldiers and townspeople in Brackett and fled to the hills where they continued their rampage, killing, raping, and robbing the homesteaders. Tye had been instrumental in the killing all of the gang and bringing Yancey in for trial. Yancey had swore he would not hang and would kill Tye the first chance he got... after having himself some fun with Tye's wife, Rebecca.

Today was the day that the outlaw was to be hung. Tye had been looking forward to this day but now that it was here, he didn't know if he was going to enjoy it or not. He had brought in a lot of men that were hung but he had never watched. Startling news came to him as he was drinking coffee in the predawn hour. This news would put himself, Rebecca, and everyone in the area in danger.

Chapter One

A n hour before first light found Tye sitting on his porch, finishing a second cup of coffee. It was late fall and the early morning air was a little on the nippy side but Tye hadn't noticed. His thoughts were focused on the coming event at noon today. Three weeks ago, he had brought the most vicious, demented criminal he had ever encountered in for trial. Yancey Cates and his gang, which included Yancey's brother, had robbed, raped, and murdered a great number of innocent homesteaders. The gang was also responsible for the death of several soldiers from Fort Clark who was friends of Tye. Yancey and his gang were ex-confederate soldiers who hated the union army and anyone who represented the United States Army was fair game to them. He was the only member of his gang left alive and he was to hang at noon today for his atrocities. Tye had been tracking down men like him for years, but Yancey was different. Most of the men he hunted down killed only when they had to, Yancey did so for the love of seeing people... men, women, and even children... suffer and die.

A great number of people had been traveling to Brackett, which was located just north of the fort, the last couple of days to watch the hanging. The town was separated from Fort Clark by the Old San Antonio/San Diego Mail Road with the fort being on the south side of the road. Word of the hanging had spread like wildfire and people were anxious to see this no account bastard hung. When Tye was with the Rangers, or Texas Mounted Rifles as some called them, he had brought in a lot of men that were hung but he had never had a desire to watch...until now. He had been looking forward to this one. When he was chasing the gang he had gotten close enough one night to listen to their talk around the campfire. He was appalled at how calloused they

1

were. They were laughing while recounting the men they had killed and the women they had raped.

'Well,' he thought, 'they are all in hell now except Yancey, and he's headed there today.' His thoughts were interrupted by Shakespeare who had opened the door and stepped out on the porch. Shakespeare had been one of the original mountain men and was best friends in those days when trapping beaver with Tye's father, Ben. Shakespeare, or Buff as he liked to be called, was seventy-one years old but one would never guess it. His eyes were clear and he moved like a man much younger. He was only about five-six and maybe 140 pounds after eating a big meal. He was lean and wiry and could still ride and shoot as well as he could forty years earlier. His face was covered by a gray, scraggly beard and his long gray hair hung to his shoulders, Indian style. The only thing that betrayed his age was his deeply lined, weathered face. He knew Ben had gotten himself killed by the Apaches awhile back and the biggest regret in life was he had never come to Texas to see his old friend. He decided to come to Fort Clark to meet his friend's son who was making quite a name for himself. He and Tye had spent a lot of time talking about Ben and those times in the Rockies. Buff never spent a day in school so he could not read or write but he could give an officer who graduated from the Point, a number of lessons that were not taught at any school in fighting Indians. He always told them with a laugh that they would be graded out here not by A's or B's but if they lived or died. If they lived, they passed until the next test and there would always be another one. He was popular among the troops not only because he represented a time they had only read about, but they loved to listen to him talk in that mountain man jargon.

He sat down on the porch next to Tye with his cup of coffee. "Hurd ya movin round making tha coffee but I wus snug in tha bed and deecided ta jus lay thar fur awhile. Still wunderin why ya want ta git out uf bed so early with that thar wife being so purty."

"Never been one to sleep late, Buff. If I stayed in bed I'd just toss and turn and wake her up."

Buff laughed. "Now, what kud be wrong with that?"

"You must be feeling a little feisty today." Tye replied laughing. Neither said anything for a couple minutes as both just sat there, drinking their coffee and waiting for the sun to break the horizon. The only sound was the babbling of nearby Los Moras Creek where it flowed around some rocks. Buff knew his friend was troubled. He broke the silence.

"Little nurvous abut tuday?"

"I know Yancey has to pay for what he's done but I'm not happy like I thought I would be about him hanging. When we first caught him, I told him I'd be on the front row, enjoying the show. Now I don't know. A kind of sick feeling is in my stomach when I think about it." Buff took another swallow of coffee thinking about what he was going to say.

"Tye, yu ar all tha gud thangs that God put inta peeple. Ole Yanc thar, he's all tha bad. Tha gud book says tha everwun has ta answer fur his life on this heer earth. It says, a man reeps whut he sows or sumthang like that. That thar man dun a lot uf bad thangs and he has ta ansur fur'um ta tha Man up stairs. Yu did this heer kuntry a big faver by bringing him in. Saved a lot uf lives."

"Didn't think you could read, Buff," Tye said smiling, thinking of the verses Buff just quoted.

"Can't, but my mama made shor she read ta us kids frum tha Bible eve'r day. Those days wur special ta me an my bruthers. Wish I knu if'n anee uf them wur still alive."

"You don't know?"

Buff sat his coffee cup down and spoke in a low, wistful voice. "No I don't. Been muving around too long and nev're got around to trackin them down. Onilest thang uther than not seeing yur pa again befor he died tha I regret."

Tye thought for a few minutes and came up with the idea that maybe the army could help Buff out and track his relatives down. He would check with Major Thurston on it. "Let's get another cup, Buff. It's still an hour or so till first light."

~~~

Yancey Cates was doing what he had been doing all night, pacing his jail cell floor. He had been sure that he would have escaped this Yankee cell by now but all his attempts had failed. Now, he was only hours from the hangman. He was upset at not escaping but more than that, his not being able to kill the man responsible for his being here…that damn scout Watkins. He and a few soldiers had killed his whole gang, including his brother. He had sworn to escape and kill Watkins the first time he saw him with no warning. 'Looks like that ain't happening,' he thought to himself. "Damn," he cursed.

"You say something, Yancey?" the guard asked.

"Go to hell you Yankee bastard!"

"I might Yancey, but guess what."

"What?"

"You're gonna beat me there," the guard said laughing and then saw a soldier coming which he figured was his relief. Walking to the soldier he stopped, startled. He did not know the man. He started to raise his rifle but the man was too quick. The 10" Bowie in his hand sliced upward catching the guard just above the belly button. The rifle was dropped as the soldier grabbed his assailant's knife hand with both of his own. He was unable to stop the man from twisting the blade and ripping it upwards, gutting him like a deer. He fell to the ground, legs twitching, and then was still.

Yancey was shocked. He didn't know what was happening.

"Yancey," came a whispered voice, then again, "Yancey."

"Here," Yancey answered. The man found the keys and unlocked the cell door.

"Let's go." The stranger ordered. As Yancey walked by the fallen soldier, he stopped and kicked him in the face. "Looks like you beat me to hell," he said laughing. He stooped and pulled a piece of paper from the soldier's pocket. He picked up a stick and using the man's blood as ink, wrote a note and laid it on the man's chest.

Outside the guardhouse, they were met by three other men. Yancey still didn't know what was going on but whatever it was sure as hell beat hanging. Nothing was said as they exited the fort by crossing the bridge over Los Moras Creek. Yancey saw the guard at the gate lying on the ground. The five men walked into Brackett and went between two buildings. Behind one of them were five horses, saddled and ready to go. Mounting up, they headed east on the Old Mail Road. No words had been spoken and Yancey was still in the dark. He thought one of the men looked familiar but no names came to him. They had their mounts headed east, intending on putting some distance between them and Fort Clark as the sun broke the horizon.

~~~

"Sorta nippy ain't it?" Buff commented sipping on his fresh cup of coffee as they sat back down on the porch. Tye just nodded his agreement.

Buff continued talking. "Mornings like these reminds me uf springtime in tha Rockies. Nites got pretty chilly even in tha summer and staed tha way till tha sun shined on yu. I kud sit here an tell yu all day abut how yur pa and me luved thos yeeres we shared in tha montons. I don't thank yu kud ever understand jus how much tha meant ta me."

"I know, Buff, and those feelings were shared by pa for you. He told me many, many times how much he loved you and even old Bridger. He said you and him were as close as any brothers could ever be."

Buff sat his empty cup down and said, "I'll tell yu sumthang, Tye. If God ever said I kud live ta be a hundert yeers old I wud tell him that if he wud allow me ta go bac to thos montons with Ben fur a short time, even a few days...I wud trade them thar yeeres. I truly wud." Tye put his hand on Buff's shoulder.

"Pa would have felt the same way." As Tye was standing up to stretch, he heard his name being called. He looked in the direction of the voice and saw a soldier running toward him, shouting. A second later, Tye recognized the soldier as his friend, Corporal Phipps.

"What in the hell you so excited about, Phipps?" Tye asked.

"HE'S GONE, TYE. HE'S GONE."

"Calm down, Phipps." Tye said putting his hand on his friend's shoulder. "Now who's gone?"

"The prisoner...he's escaped."

"YOU MEAN YANCEY?" Tye shouted.

"Yes Sir. He and some other men knifed a guard and escaped."

"WHEN?"

"Just in the last few minutes, Tye."

Dammit to hell," Tye said angrily. "Buff, get your gun and get inside. I know that man is going to try to get to me through Rebecca. I'm going to Thurston." He turned to leave then turned back to Buff. "He's as bad as there is, Buff. Don't hesitate to shoot. Please... take care of her till I get back."

"Kount on it, Tye. Don't ya wurry nune abut her. Now. Git goin'."

"I'll stay here too if you want, Tye," Phipps said.

"Thanks, Phipps. Just be careful. You have no idea how depraved this man is so shoot first and ask questions later." Tye left to see Thurston, the Post Commander. He hadn't gone fifty feet when he saw the major headed his way with four men. Before they met, Thurston was giving orders to the men.

"Lacy, you and Meeks take the front and Jackson, you and Kent take the back." Thurston said nodding toward the house. The men sprinted to take up their positions. "DON'T HESITATE TO SHOOT," he hollered at them. "Let's go inside, Tye," he said as they passed Phipps who was on the porch. Inside, they found Rebecca sitting at the table with Buff. Buff and Thurston acknowledged each other and Thurston turned to Rebecca.

"You are as beautiful in the morning as you are in the evening, Rebecca."

"Thank you, Major. That is quite nice of you to say even though we both know it's not true," she said laughing. She saw the troubled look on Tye's face as she turned to him to say good morning. "What's going on?" she asked? Tye started to answer but Thurston spoke up as he sat down at the table. Buff had poured everyone a cup of coffee. The major didn't beat around the bush but told her and Tye what happened.

"Yancey escaped a little while ago." Rebecca looked at Tye who nodded his acknowledgement that it was true. She had an alarmed look on her face as she sat there looking at her husband. She reached over and took Tye's hand.

"Two guards were killed," Thurston said; "the guard at the guardhouse and the guard at the bridge."

"Did either say anything?" Tye asked.

"The guard at the gate came around just before he died. He said there was at least four and one was in uniform."

"UNIFORM?" Tye cried out... "That means another soldier is dead somewhere."

Thurston nodded.

"We're looking now."

"Did the guard say anything else?" Tye asked... Thurston looked at Rebecca. "Go ahead and say it," Tye said, knowing what was coming.

"The guard at the guard house died before saying anything but this was lying on his chest." He handed the note to Tye, looked at Rebecca and then lowered his eyes to the floor. Thurston cleared his throat. "He wanted you to know he was coming but before he killed you he..." he stopped, looking down at his coffee cup.

"He's gonna get Rebecca first...right?" Tye said. Thurston didn't look up for a second, only nodding his head. Rebecca stood up, turning over her chair and ran around the table to Tye who was already up. They held each other for a moment. Tye spread the piece of paper out on the table. The writing was not legible and was hard to make out the words. Rebecca was reading over Tye's shoulder.

She asked. "What kind of ink is that he used?"

Tye turned his head to look at her and answered. "It's not ink, honey; it's the guard's blood that was knifed." She had a horrible, disgusted expression on her face and turned away holding her hand over her mouth. Tye embraced her, pulling her tight against his chest.

"Everything is going to be okay, honey," he said. "It's going to be okay." She sat down and Tye read the note again.

Watkins, I told yu I wusn't gonna be hung, You better be looking over your shoulder cause I'm gonna kill you right after I have me sum fun with that purty wife of yours. Yancey.

Thurston, standing up, said, "I will take responsibility for Rebecca, Tye. He will have to kill every damn man on the fort before he gets to her. I will have at least four men here during the day and double that at night. Between them and Buff, things should be okay."

"I appreciate that Major. Give me a few minutes with Buff and Rebecca and then I'll see you at headquarters." Thurston walked out the door, made sure Lacy and Meeks were where they were supposed to be. As he stepped off the porch, Tye spoke to him from the door.

"Can you get a patrol together?"

"Already done, Tye"

"What about Captain McClellan or Lieutenant Garrison can one..."

"Both already volunteered Tye, as well as Christian and Phipps over there."

7

He paused, "to be truthful, every damn officer, non-com, and enlisted man on the post wanted to go. I practically had to put shackles on Corporal Arnold. He hasn't fully recovered from his wounds yet, but wanted to go. I've got you the four I mentioned plus six others including your scout, Dan August. They are saddled and ready to go with supplies for a week. They're just waiting for you." He turned back and headed for headquarters.

Rebecca, tears rolling down her cheeks, hugged Tye. "Do you have to go?" she sobbed. Tye placed his hand on her chin and turned her face up and kissed her on the lips. Her lips were hot and slightly salty from the tears. He pulled back, looking down at her.

"I've got to, honey. If he's not caught he's gonna kill a lot of innocent people. I couldn't live with that." He turned to Buff. "I've got to count on you to keep her safe, Buff. Until I get back so don't leave her alone for a minute."

Buff nodded his head. "Kount on it, Tye. Now go git tha bastard." He stuck out his hand to shake, which Tye shook. "Don't yu wurry nun abut her," he said keeping his grip on Tye's hand. "Nun at all," he repeated.

"Thanks, Buff." Turning back to Rebecca he said he had to gather up what he needed and would be right back. He went inside and Rebecca sat down on the porch with Buff sitting down beside her. She put her head on his shoulder. She loved the way he smelled because it reminded her of her father. She missed him and her mother. They had been killed several months earlier and she had come to Fort Clark to live with her dad's brother, Master Sergeant O'Malley, and his wife. They were very loving and she quickly became attached to them. Sergeant O'Malley introduced her to Tye who was Chief of Scouts at Cark.

She had heard stories about this young scout that were hard to believe. It didn't take her long to find out they were mostly true. He was a strikingly handsome man. His hair was coal black and fell almost to his shoulders, Indian style. His face was dark, tanned from the years he spent under the sun. His eyes were deep blue and had the crowfeet wrinkles in the corners, as most did out here, the result of squinting so much because of the burning sun. He had a mustache that matched the hair on his head. His shoulders were broad and his arms were like cord wood. There was no fat on him and yet, he had almost a hundred ninety pounds stacked on his six-two frame. He was the most handsome man she had ever met and she fell in love with him immediately. He was tough, meaner than an Apache when need be, but was tender in his loving with her. She raised her head and looked back when the door opened and Tye walked out.

He had gone through his metamorphosis. He had removed his pressed pants, blue shirt, and polished boots. He had his faded blue cavalry pants on, his Apache moccasin boots that came up almost to his knees, his revolver on his right hip, the Sharps rifle in his left hand, and his Bowie stuck in the top of his right boot. He had his buckskin shirt on which he never took off while on patrol. It had belonged to his father and he would never part with it…it was part of him. On his head was his faded, sweat-stained gray cavalry hat. He had a worn, fringed leather jacket thrown over his shoulder in case one of the unexpected Texas cold spells set in.

Rebecca stood up and leaned against him. "Be careful, darling…come back to me."

"I've told you before," Tye said smiling, "there's nothing that would keep me from coming back to you." He kissed her on the forehead and as he turned to leave spoke to Buff. "I'm counting on you, Buff. He's made his threats and I take them seriously. He's as bad as they come." Buff nodded as he and a tearful Rebecca watched Tye walk away.

~~~

Yancey, resting his mount, looked back over his shoulder. He could see no dust indicating they were being pursued. "Let's give the horses a blow," he said to his friends. Since leaving Brackett they had covered about five miles on the Old Mail Road and then cut north. They were now about two miles off the road. Yancey knew it would be hard to decipher their tracks on the road because of the number of people traveling on it. He knew the scouts would be looking north and south of the road for tracks showing if they left the road. He felt pretty safe because where they left the road; they had followed the tracks of a herd of goats, their horse's tracks mixing in with theirs. He figured they could rest for thirty or so minutes and then head a few miles farther from the road and make camp.

He looked at the men. "Do I know you?"

"Probably not," the taller of the four said. "We were in the same outfit as you for a short period of time. We," then he corrected himself, "That is all of us except Mitch there with the uniform on, were taken prisoner about six months before the war ended. After the war ended, we just sorta drifted and ended up in San Antonio. That's where we were when we heard about your hanging, or fixing to be hung I should say. We just couldn't see letting a good old southern boy be hung by the damn Yankees."

They all shook hands after the introductions. The five of them all had one thing in common… a hate for the Union. Yancey looked at the man with the uniform, the one named Mitch.

"You best get out of that damn blue uniform or I might just have to kill you," he said laughing. Mitch got up, stripped the uniform off and took some clothes out of his saddlebag.

While sitting there; Yancey's thoughts drifted to Watkins. He intended to make Tye's dying a painful one and then take his pleasure with his wife that he had heard was so pretty. 'Hell,' he thought, 'I might just pleasure myself with her in front of him before I kill them both.' He laughed at the thought of Tye struggling and his misery of watching something like that.

"I'm a little hungry," Yancey commented to no one in particular. None of the men said anything. "Ya'll did bring some supplies didn't you?" Again no one said anything, just looking at each other. Yancey stood up; towering over the men squatted on the ground.

"YOU MEAN TO TELL ME YOU DID NOT GET SUPPLIES?" he yelled.

"Calm down, Yancey," Logan said. "Just calm down for a minute. No, we didn't think to get supplies. We got to Brackett about three a.m. and there's not too many stores open anywhere at that time. We had just enough time to stable our horses, feed them, and then get some rest before breaking you out. The owner of the stable was up because, he said, so damn many people were coming in for the hanging and had to stable their horses it was impossible to get any sleep. Said, he would be glad when that bastard was hung so he could get some rest."

"The damn man can identify you," Yancey remarked.

"Naw he won't," Mitch replied. "He's sleeping now…permanently."

"Well, at least you did one thing right," Yancey remarked.

"Not very appreciative are you, Yancey?" Tom commented. "The least you could do would be to show a little appreciation for us keeping you from your date with the hangman." Yancey, sitting back down, was quite for a moment then spoke up...

"You're right, Tom. I guess I was a little off base with that comment. Been wondering about something though; where did you get the army uniform Mitch was wearing?'

"Poor old soldier boy should of stayed at the fort instead of getting drunk at the saloon in town. We killed him when he was staggering back to the fort."

"You sure that the soldiers can't follow us?" Tom asked. "I heard about this scout that can track a fish in water."

"Yeah, I heard all that crap about him," Yancey answered.

"Isn't he the one who brought you in?" Mitch asked.

"The same," Yancey answered. "I intend to kill him and take my pleasure with his wife."

"You're not thinking of going back to Clark and doing this are you?" Logan queried

"Been thinking of nothing else ever since he put me in that stinking cell. That note I left told him I was coming for him." The four men were dumbfounded. They were too amazed at his brashness to say anything.

Yancey, seeing the look on their faces, asked "What's the problem with that?"

Mitch spoke up. "I think I can speak for the four of us when I say you are crazy. That *damn scout* as you call him has a reputation all over the country. Hell, we listened to stories about some of the things he did when we were in San Antonio. That's how we heard about you. I for one, and I think the others also, had just as well leave him alone and just be satisfied you escaped the hangman."

"I DON'T GIVE A DAMN WHAT YOU THINK!" Yancey exclaimed loudly, standing up. "You can come with me or go your own way. I don't care one way or another but that stinking scout is gonna pay for what he did to me. Besides, he killed my brother." He mounted his horse, looked over his shoulder and started to ride away when Grant grabbed his reins.

"Settle down some, Yancey. Just relax a little. Mitch didn't mean we wasn't going to go with you. Let's just get a plan together and not

11

go rushing into anything. He's right about this man, Watkins, so let's not do anything rash."

"Alright," Yancey said dismounting, "we'll talk about it." He walked his horse over to where the others were picketed.

The four of them had stood up at Yancey's outburst. Now, they sat back down and watched him picket his horse.

"He's full of hate isn't he?" Grant committed more of a statement rather than a question. "Never would have said thanks or nothing else about our saving his neck if Tom hadn't mentioned it."

"As far as I'm concerned, he can go get killed by himself." Mitch said.

"Let's just camp here awhile, get some rest and sort things out" Logan said.

"Don't you think the army will be after us?" Mitch asked.

"They won't be able to find our tracks because of all the others on that road, so just relax." Logan stated.

Yancey came back to the group, his anger gone. "Don't guess I told you boys, but I appreciate you getting me out of that damn guard house." The four just nodded their heads and smiled. "You're welcome," Tom said slapping him on the shoulder when Yancey sat down beside him.

"Mitch, if you will start a fire I'll get the coffee and we'll take us a breather for awhile and talk things out." Mitch mumbled something under his breath that no one understood, but got up and started gathering some wood. Logan gathered some rocks and made a circle with them to build the fire in.

"Keep it small," Grant said, "We don't need to advertise where we are with a lot of smoke." After the fire was going and the coffee made, everyone was relaxed, drinking their coffee. Mitch got up and walked off a ways to answer natures call.

"Where did ya'll pick him up?" Yancey asked.

"In San Antonio about a month ago" Logan said. "Old Grant there got himself into some trouble during a card game with two locals. They were pulling down on Logan when Mitch stepped in and killed both of them with bullets square thru the heart. Fastest I ever did see when he pulled that gun."

"I'd been dead fur sure if he hadn't," Grant said.

"If he didn't know you, why did he step in?" Yancey asked.

Tom spoke up. "Said he had played with them the day before. Thought they were cheating but couldn't figure out how. He lost a little money to them. He was watching them while they were playing Grant and saw one of them deal from the bottom. Grant saw it too and he called the man a damn cheat. They both stood up and was pulling their guns out when Mitch stepped in." He laughed and added, "When he shot them, he walked over to the table and told everyone they were cheats, that he had lost thirty dollars to them the day before. He picked up thirty dollars off the table, asked Grant how much he lost and took it from the two men's pile and handed it to Grant. There was still a lot of money on the table. He turned to the crowd that was watching and told them he didn't figure the two would need the rest and they were welcome to it. There was a hell of rush for the money. Ole Grant got knocked plumb out of his chair and damn near got stomped to death," he said laughing.

"What about the law?"

"Wasn't no problem, Yancey. Everyone saw the two draw down on Grant. Mitch just prevented a murder."

"Amen to that," Grant said. "I thought I was dead meat." Mitch came back and sat down.

"What about this scout, Yancey? You've seen him. Are the stories true?" Mitch asked.

"Probably what you boys heard was true." The four of them were caught off guard at the statement because most stories about men out here were stretched a mite. "He's tough, I'll say that. He's well over six feet tall and built like a damn blacksmith. He's smart and hell on wheels in a fight. Beat the hell out of me and I ain't no pilgrim when it comes to a stand up knock'um down fist fight. When the soldier boys that were bringing me in were ambushed in a canyon, he escaped and must have run forty miles on foot to bring help. He saved our asses from a very painful death."

"We heard about that; didn't believe no white man could have done that." Logan said shaking his head.

"Well, he did exactly that. I think the sonofabitch is more Apache than white."

"Do you think it wise then to go after him and his wife?" Mitch asked. Yancey's eyes were cold as ice when he answered and Mitch's insides froze from looking at them.

"He's responsible for my brother's death. He was responsible for Lance's and all the rest of my friends getting killed. You damn right he's gonna pay and I'm gonna get a hell of lot of satisfaction in watching him die."

Chapter Two

Tye and the patrol were three miles east of Brackett on the Old Mail Road. Tye knew there would be no way they could follow the men with all the tracks on the road... unless they cut off the road. He figured they would before they got to Uvalde where Fort Inge was located. If he was one of them, he wouldn't want to be around any soldiers right now if he could help it. The patrol was moving slowly down the road and Tye was on the south side of the road and his best scout, August, was on the north side. They were looking for fresh tracks leaving the road. He pulled Sandy up when August whistled. He rode quickly across the road to where he was.

"What do you have, Dan?"

"A hell of lot of tracks... goat tracks."

"Goat tracks?" Tye asked, kind of bewildered why Dan called him over.

"Yeah, goat tracks with fresh horse tracks mixed in." Both dismounted to take a closer look.

"No more than an hour or two old," Dan said, tracing one of the tracks with his finger. Tye stood up and looked in the direction the tracks headed.

"Five sets of tracks," Tye said. "It has to be them but why in hell are they headed north? There's nothing in that direction."

"There's some homesteaders," Dan said. Tye didn't say anything; he was staring off in the distance. Finally he spoke.

"Is that smoke?" he asked, pointing with his Sharps. Dan looked where he was pointing.

"I'll be damned. If that ain't a campfire I'll eat my hat."

"That's what I figure too. Pretty stupid if it's them." They mounted their horses and rode over to where Captain McClellan and the patrol waited.

"What did you find?" McClellan asked.

15

"Looks like they left the road and headed north; at least we think it's them. No way to be sure, but there's five sets of tracks. There's a campfire about two, two and half miles yonder," Tye said pointing.

McClellan stood up in his stirrups and looked where Tye pointed. He could see the smoke only after staring for a few seconds in the direction that Tye was pointing. How in blazes those two scouts spotted it, he didn't know. It wasn't the first time he had appreciated their special talent. They seemed to sense trouble before it happened. In fact, only one patrol, out of no telling how many that Tye has led, had been ambushed and he had warned McClellan he had a feeling there was trouble there. It was McClellan's call to go into the canyon but Tye still felt responsible for it. Tye, and men like him, were a special breed, born to do this because one can't develop that special sense…you have it or you don't. Most men don't. Tye learned the physical part of scouting, the tracking and fighting, from his father, Ben. Ben had stories written about him in the dime novels that were so popular back east. Now, his son was making a name for himself. He was known all over this part of Texas as the best scout in the army. He was loved by the troopers and the homesteaders, feared by the bandits and respected as a great warrior by the Apaches. Among the Apache, he was big medicine and to kill him would raise a warrior's status to great heights.

"Is it their camp?" McClellan asked.

"Probably not," Dan answered.

"One thing about things out here," Tye said. "Don't ever think something is as it should be. The minute you think you know what is or is gonna be, things are just the opposite. Thinking like that can get a man killed. Best be prepared for anything all the time." Tye turned in the saddle and looked back where the smoke was. "If it's okay with you, Captain, Dan and me will take a look and see what we have there. As much noise as the patrol makes we'd never get close to them." McClellan nodded his approval. The two men turned their mounts and headed toward the smoke, leaving McClellan and the patrol.

McClellan watched them go. He sat there leaning forward, his hands on the pommel of his saddle. The position took some weight off his butt and it felt good. As he watched Tye ride away he thought back to this past summer when Tye had ridden to his rescue after his stupidity had gotten his patrol ambushed. Until that moment, he hated

16

Tye...and for no reason other than pure jealousy. Tye had all the respect one could expect from the enlisted men and other officers and especially, Major Thurston. McClellan had none. He had not been tested in battle on any of the patrols he had led. When he finally had the chance, he gave an order that got himself and his men ambushed and several killed. He was feeling ashamed, embarrassed and as low as the belly of a snake. He wanted a career in the army, maybe someday be a general. After the ambush, he figured the general idea was out and that he might be busted back to a lieutenant or lower... even ousted from the army altogether.

Tye had pulled him aside and talked at length with him. He told him everyone makes mistakes and the one he had made was the most frequent and to forget it and learn from it. He said the men saw him fight valiantly and they would respect him for that. Tye then told the men later that McClellan was going to be a good officer and gave other examples of officers that made the same mistake and had turned into real fighting men and damn good officers. McClellan could not believe that Tye did not tell Thurston about it. He did not know Tye had not told the major until he gave his own report on the battle to the major. Tye had not only saved his life but his career. He would always be appreciative of that and no one had his respect more than Tye.

"We'd better get going, Sir." Norwood said quietly. His voice brought McClellan back to reality.

He stood in his stirrups, twisted his body to look back at the men and gave the order, "Forward Yo," and they moved out, making sure they kept a good quarter of mile distance behind Tye.

After a few minutes trotting their horses, Tye and Dan slowed them to a walk. Sound carries a long ways and the land here was rocky, making it impossible for the horses to move quietly. When they figured they were three hundred yards from the camp, they dismounted, hobbled their mounts and moved quietly toward the fire. Both men wore their moccasin boots and they moved with no sound other than the rustle of mesquite limbs brushing their clothes and it was no louder than a whisper. There was a slight breeze from the southwest so they moved to the right of the camp, figuring on coming in against the breeze to keep what noise they did make from being carried to the men. Also, if there was talk in the camp, the breeze would carry their voices to them.

They worked their way to the edge of the camp and watched, hidden by the thick mesquite. They could see the men clearly.

"There's five of them and that one sitting to the right is Yancey," Tye whispered. "If we try and take them now there's gonna be some dead men, maybe one or both of us included. Why don't you skedaddle back to McClellan and get them up here...quietly. I'll watch them."

"Be back in twenty or so minutes." Dan scooted back from the brush a few feet and then ran in a crouch to his horse. Yancey had seen the movement out of the corner of his eye.

"Don't turn your heads or stand up or do anything foolish," Yancey whispered to the men.

"Wh...What is it?" Logan asked knowing something was wrong. Yancey set down his coffee and slowly stood to his feet and stretched. In a low voice and as nonchalant as he could, he spoke to the men.

"Don't look around. We've got company, boys. Just stand up slow like and put out the fire and mosey over to our horses. Just act like nothing is wrong."

Grant, understanding what was happening played it to the hilt. In a loud voice he said, "That blonde over at the saloon was something else. How about it Mitch? You were there after I was."

"Best I ever had," Mitch answered laughing, fumbling with his cinch on the saddle with his trembling hands.

Tye was cursing his luck. If he tried to take them alone he would surely die. There was no way he could cut down five of them. He might lower the odds some though. He checked his sharps for clogging as he always does after crawling along the ground. Several years ago, he had seen a young ranger get half his face blown away by a clogged barrel. It made a lasting impression on him. He figured he could drop one of them when they rode off...if he was lucky, maybe two. He pulled his colt and decided he would take the close shot with it and the longer one with the Sharps. Each of the outlaws was mounted and on a command from Yancey, spurred their mounts. They were riding directly away from Tye, maybe thirty or forty yards away. Tye was a crack shot and aimed at the last rider's back and squeezed the trigger. The Colt jumped in his hand and he saw the man grab his shoulder but stayed in the saddle. Cursing at himself, Tye quickly grabbed his Sharps and slowly applied pressure to the trigger. He saw another man jerk when the bullet hit him. He stayed in the saddle for a couple strides then fell off, hitting the ground hard, flopping like a rag doll. Tye had seen many men knocked off their mounts and knew immediately by the way he hit the ground he was dead. He felt a little remorse at shooting the man in the back but he really had no choice. He couldn't let all of them get away. He was glad for one thing though; glad it wasn't Yancey because a quick bullet was too good for him.

He could hear the patrol approaching in a hurry because of the shots. Dan arrived first with McClellan hot on his heels. Both were relieved when Tye stood up and waved.

"WHAT HAPPENED?" McClellan shouted as his horse sat down on his haunches, sliding to a stop.

"They must have spotted Dan as he was coming back to you. They jumped on their horses and headed hell bent for leather west."

"You okay," Dan asked.

"Better than a couple of them. One's down over yonder," he said nodding toward where the man had went down, "and another is laying low in the saddle with a bullet in the shoulder."

"McClellan yelled, "SERGEANT NORWOOD."

Norwood came in a hurry. "Yes Sir."

"There's a man down over there," McClellan said pointing in the direction Tye had nodded. "Get a man and bring him over here."

"Yes Sir." Norwood turned in the saddle, "Lightfoot and Hill, you two find that body and get it over here."

"Yes Sir," Lightfoot shouted as he and Mason dismounted and ran over to find the body. About a minute later, Mason shouted they had found him.

"Deader than a old piece of wood, Sergeant." Hill said as they dropped the body by Norwood's feet.

Norwood nodded, "You two get remounted and see if you can find his horse."

"Yo!" Both said at the same time.

Tye and McClellan kneeled down beside the man and went through his pockets trying to find something to identify him. They found some tobacco and makings and about six dollars. The two men arrived leading the man's horse.

"Throw me the saddle bags," McClellan said. Lightfoot tossed them to him. Inside was a shirt, jacket, pants, and some jerky. "He was a

19

corporal," McClellan said tossing the Confederate jacket to Tye. Tye caught the coat and rummaged through the pockets.

"Nothing," Tye said.

"That guy had less than I do." Private Hill said laughing.

"Barely," Lightfoot said. McClellan's head jerked up.

"That's enough you two. Quit your joking around. A man's dead here."

Tye walked over to where the man had fallen and looked in the direction the men had headed. McClellan walked over to him.

"What are you thinking, Tye?" Tye squatted down on his haunches, picked up a twig and began chewing on it...thinking. McClellan waited patiently. He knew this man never made a rash statement. Everything he said was thought out

"They're headed to the mountains north of Brackett. There's water and game there."

"Are they going to get help for the wounded man?"

Tye spit the twig out and laughed. "Not this bunch, Captain. They will let him suffer and die of infection before they do that. If they can find a camp and feel safe, they may try to fix him up themselves but they won't go near a place where there would be a doctor. I think we had better get after them and not give them that chance." McClellan nodded.

"My feelings too. SERGEANT NORWOOD."

"Here, Sir."

"Have the men get to their mounts and move out."

"Yes Sir." Norwood walked toward the men and repeated the order. "Get to your mounts and prepare to move out."

"Yo" came from several men. When mounted, they moved out two abreast with Tye and Dan galloping out to their usual position, a quarter mile in front. The tracks were not hard to follow so Tye was spending more time watching the trail ahead for signs of ambush than looking at the tracks. He figured them being southern boys, they were probably crack shots with a rifle. The terrain here was gently rolling hills with an arroyo here and there, causing a detour or two. He could see the mountains ahead of him, maybe twenty miles farther. They were shrouded in a blue haze. He knew the southern edge of this small mountain range was no more than twenty or so miles north of Brackett,

Fort Clark...and Rebecca. Unconsciously, he picked up the pace a little.

~~~

Yancey and the others pulled up to give their horses a blow. As one, they all turned and looked at their back trail, hoping like hell they saw no one. They saw the dust.

"How in hell's name did they catch up to us that quick?" Grant asked.

"Had to have been that damn scout," Tom replied.

"Don't start talking like that man is something he's not. He will bleed just like me and you." Yancey added.

"Well, Logan's probably dead and Mitch has a hole in his shoulder. What's the plan MR. YANCEY?" Tom asked a touch of sarcasm in his voice. Yancey jerked his head around. Logan's insides turned to ice. Yancey's eyes were as dead as Logan's, no sign of any emotion.

"We will find a camp, get some rest and then we'll make plans in the morning. Right now, I need time to figure this out. Get Mitch on his horse and let's move out." Tom and Grant helped the wounded man on his horse despite the man's protest. He was hurting something fierce and cussed his bad luck. Yancey was out in front by about fifty yards.

"That damn Yancey is crazier than hell," Mitch moaned. "Going back to the Fort like that just to get even with that scout and his wife is the stupidest thing I ever heard tell."

"I agree, but are you gonna argue with him. Hell, he'd kill his own mother if she crossed him," Tom said, keeping his voice low.

"Biggest damn mistake we ever made was getting that sonofabitch out of the hanging. It was the stupidest thing we ever did. He's gonna get us all shot... or hung," Grant said, adding his two-bits worth.

"This damn piece of lead has got to come out...and quick," Mitch said, sweat rolling down his face... a face grimacing in pain with every step his mount took.

"I'll do it when we make camp," Grant promised.

21

Gary McMillan

Chapter Three

The shadows were becoming long as Tye made his way around another arroyo. There was less than an hour of sunlight left and hope of catching up to the outlaws this day were pretty slim. The tracks showed the men had slowed, probably looking for a place to camp. He pulled Sandy up as he topped a small hill. Looking back over his shoulder, he could see the patrol coming about three hundred yards away. Turning back, he stared at the lone mountain off to his left that was just six or so miles north of Fort Clark. Looking straight ahead, he could see the hill country no more than five miles away. These were mountains to Texans. A man could not compare them to the ones found in the Rockies. That's what Buff said. Tye chuckled to himself thinking about when Buff bent over double laughing at what we called mountains. He hooked his leg over his saddle horn, took the makings out of his shirt pocket and rolled himself a smoke while waiting on the patrol. He figured they had better make camp pretty quick. There would be no moon tonight and it would be getting dark soon.

McClellan and the patrol arrived. "Anything wrong?"

"No Sir. Just thought we might think about making camp. It's going to be dark soon."

McClellan turned to Sergeant Norwood who was riding right behind him. "Tell the men we are camping here. Set the pickets, the latrines, and the schedule for the sentries."

"Right away Captain. Will it be a cold camp?"

McClellan looked at Tye who just shrugged his shoulders indicating it was okay either way. "Tell the men they are to have small fires to cook their food and boil some coffee. The fires are to be put out before full dark."

"Yes Sir," Norwood said smiling. "Hot food just naturally makes a soldier in a better mood," he said as he walked off. In less than twenty minutes the camp was set, a fire started, and the aroma of fresh coffee

23

boiling filled the camp. Norwood had set the sentry schedule, horses picketed, and latrines dug. Men filtered into the firelight with their coffee cups. A large skillet was brought from the pack horse and placed on rocks that were around the fire. The men threw some bacon in to fry, and then placed biscuits in to soak up some of the grease. Hot, greasy biscuits and fried bacon made a sandwich that only a soldier could appreciate.

A private, that Tye recognized but did not know his name, sat down beside him. He chewed on the biscuit and washed it down with the coffee.

"Tye," he said. "Been wondering why you do what you do. God knows it's probably the most dangerous job on this here frontier. I know you can read some, write, and do numbers which is more than I can say for me and most of these here sorry-ass soldiers I ride with," he said sweeping his arm toward the other men sitting around the fire and laughing. The others were laughing and someone hit him with a small rock. "With a wife as pretty as Rebecca I just…" Tye interrupted him.

"This is my country out here. I didn't get assigned or move out here, I was born here and I love it. I despise those that try to destroy this country and appreciate the good people that's struggling to make a go of it."

"Like the Apache?" someone asked.

"No, not the Apache, just the low life, lazy bastards that come in here to take what other men have worked for," Tye said looking at the private. "If you, your father, your grandfather, and his father had lived in this land would you not consider it your land? That's how I feel about the Apache. They are simply trying to preserve their way of life. I was brought up by a man that taught me a lot of things like tracking and fighting, but most important, teaching me to respect this land and the people that live here. Sure pa fought them just as I have, but he never hated them. I was taught that a man was judged on how he did his job, if he kept his word, and never shirked a job or responsibility. If you did these things it didn't make a tinkers damn where you came from or what you had done it the past. I do what I do not only because I love it, but because I feel it is what I was born to do…my destiny so to speak."

A soldier spoke that Tye did not know. "Sounds to me like you admire these heathens."

Tye looked at the man and spoke with no malice in his voice even though he was agitated at the implication.

"Are you referring to the bandits or the Apaches? There are more heathen whites than Apache." The soldier had a disbelieving look on his face. Tye continued speaking. "The Apache believe in one God. They don't worship the same God we do but they do believe in Ussen. Ussen is their One-God, their creator that they worship. All Apaches believe in their God which is more than I can say for the white race. They are an honorable people. They will not steal from another Apache in their tribe. A warrior can leave his camp and be gone for a day, two days, or a month and his belongings in his wickiup will be as he left them when he returns. Even the most vicious of the warriors are gentle with their children. Adultery is taboo and is not tolerated, often ending with the guilty party being put to death or banished from the tribe. Can you say that about all white men?" No one spoke knowing that the soldier had just been chastised by Tye, but in a very diplomatic way.

"I do believe that is more words than I have heard you speak in the last month," Garrison said smiling.

"Hell, Lieutenant," Phipps added, "I've known him for over a year and never knew he was so eloquent. His usual response is a grunt or maybe two or three words. I'm impressed," he said laughing.

"Well then, starting now, that's all you two will get," Tye replied laughing as everyone else was.

"Let's get some shut eye," McClellan said rolling out his bedroll. There was the sound of other bedrolls being unrolled and men grunting and moaning as they lay on the rocky ground, trying to get comfortable. The only sounds in a few minutes were the horses munching their oats, snoring men and the footfalls of the sentries as they walked the perimeter of the camp.

An owl screeched as he flew low over the camp looking for his supper. Tye, sitting up on his bedroll, noticed the sky to the north had some heavy clouds with a little lightning. It was a long ways off and was north, so he wasn't concerned as very few storms came in from that direction. He lay down and thought of Rebecca. He knew every man envied him because of her, and he knew he was the luckiest man around to have her as his wife. Not only was she beautiful, but smart and thoughtful of others. She was a damn good cook too on top of everything else. The only other woman that had been as pretty as her was Lori, his mother. She was quite a lady. When pa met her in San Antonio she was working in a clothes store. Her folks were against her marrying Ben at first, but quickly saw that it was like butting their heads against a wall. When they married, they built a homestead close to the Rio Grande in 1837. It was about forty or so miles south and west of where Fort Clark was built years later. Ben knew how to survive and we were never hungry. Never had no money but who needed it. We grew vegetables, had chickens and goats, a few cows and there was a lot of game. We were very happy there. An owl sitting somewhere nearby in a tree screeched and in the distance, a coyote's lonely, mournful howl could be heard. Tye rolled over on his side and quickly went to sleep.

~~~

Mitch, lying on his bedroll knew he was fixing to be in some serious pain. He looked at the knife Grant held just at the top of the flames on the small fire they had made.

"Be ready in a minute," Grant said to no one in particular. He was sure the blade was sterilized so he stood up and walked over to Mitch who could not take his eyes off the blade.

"Yo…You don…you done this before?" he stammered, looking up at Grant's face. Grant kneeled down beside his friend.

"No, Mitch, I haven't. But it's got to be done and done now before infection sets in and then it's too late. We both seen it a lot during the war."

"Yeah, I know that, but it's a hell of lot different when it's you getting cut on."

He took a piece of rawhide that Tom handed him. "Let's get it done," he said putting the rawhide stick between his teeth.

"Try to hold him as still as possible," Grant said to Tom. Grant straddled Mitch's chest and Tom, kneeling behind Mitch's head pressed down on the good shoulder and held the other arm flat on the ground. "Ready, Mitch?" Grant asked.

Mitch, biting down on the rawhide nodded his head and shut his eyes. When the point of the blade entered the hole his eyes flew open and his face turned plum red but he didn't utter a sound. Sweat rolled down his face and as Grant probed deeper, his eyes were bulging and he was rolling his head back and forth. Tom held tight.

"I FOUND IT," Grant hollered excitedly. A second later, he pulled the lead out and laid it on Mitch's chest. Mitch nodded and patted his friend on the shoulder, relaxed and lay his head back down. Two seconds later he screamed as Tom poured whiskey into the wound.

"You got to close that hole, Grant," Tom said. Grant already had the blade in the fire waiting for it to start glowing red. When it did, he scooted back over to Mitch. "This is gonna hurt some, but it's got to be done."

"DAMN," Mitch screamed as the blade was moved across the hole. The smell of burnt flesh filled the men's nostrils as the flesh melted, covering the hole.

"Done," Grant said.

"He's passed out," Tom said.

"Best thing for him. He'll feel a hell of lot better when he wakes up." They both suddenly scrambled for their guns at the sound of an approaching horse.

"It's me... Yancey." They both holstered their guns and stood up. Yancey came into the firelight, dismounted and looked down at Mitch.

"We got the bullet out," Tom said, "but he passed out." Yancey just nodded and picked up the bottle of whiskey and sat down.

"You two get some rest. I'll take the first watch."

~~~

Major Thurston walked back into his office. It was dark and he was concerned. He had been to Tye's house checking the sentries for the third time today. He had tripled the sentries along Los Moras Creek which was the eastern and southern border of the Fort and close to Tye's home. Fort Clark, like so many other forts along the frontier had no walls. The major wasn't concerned that anyone would enter the fort any other place because of the distance they would have to walk to get to Tye's home. There were too many sentries and they would be stopped and questioned. He had given the order that no civilians would be allowed on the fort until he said different... If trouble came, it would be from the creek. He had six men walking the creek and four around the house.

Thurston was sitting at his desk when his orderly and everyone else left for the evening. He leaned back in his chair, closed his eyes and relaxed. His mind drifted back to the happy times he shared with his wife. That was before he accepted the assignment at Clark. He had been a war hero and was the toast of Washington. Any assignment that was available, he could have had. When he accepted the assignment at Clark, his wife and mother cried for three straight days. They could not believe he wanted an assignment on the frontier and certainly not in Texas where there was nothing but sand and cactus. His wife lasted only a few weeks at Clark. There was no restaurants, no stores to shop, and no entertainment except listening to the boring gossip of the officer's wives. When she left she took part of Thurston with her.

Since that time he had put all his efforts in making the area around Clark safe for the flood of homesteaders settling along the Border of Mexico. Not only was he putting his efforts into that, but he was laying plans for buildings on the fort built from rocks and mortar from the quarry located on the northwest corner of the fort, close to the spring. He wanted to put up buildings that would stand the test of time instead of wood and adobe as they were now.

He was the first at headquarters in the mornings and usually the last to leave in the evening. He had the respect of his officers, non-commission officers, and the enlisted men. He leaned forward in his chair and flipped quickly through the paper work on his desk, making sure no new correspondence had come in. Standing up, he blew out the lamp and finally left for his home, feeling like everything was under control.

~~~

Rebecca had seldom left her home since Tye left and when she did, Buff stuck closer to her than a tick on a hound dog. She was anxious for this to be over so they could get back to a normal life. Buff slept a lot during the day and was at the table drinking coffee all through the night with his Bowie and Sharps on the table. He told her he figured if trouble came, it would be at night. He also made sure the sentries were aware of that.

Sergeant O'Malley visited frequently and Mrs. O'Malley was there every day, keeping Rebecca company. Ever since Rebecca had come to live with them, Mrs. O'Malley had treated her like a daughter. She seemed to always know exactly the right thing to say to cheer Rebecca up, or to squelch her fears about Tye when he was gone. Rebecca felt no fear for herself but she knew if trouble came, the soldiers and Buff would be in harm's way. She did not want anyone hurt, especially Buff, so she decided to stay indoors as much as possible. The nights were the worse when Tye was gone as now. She usually found sleep hard to come by because of her thoughts of Tye and wanting him in bed beside her. She missed his tender embraces. She prayed to God every night for his protection of Tye, and to lead him back to her. She had many things to be thankful for in her life but finding Tye was the top of the list. He was by far the best thing that ever happened to her. She rolled over, hugged Tye's pillow to her breast and cried herself to sleep.

Gary McMillan

Chapter Four

The early morning sun found Tye kneeling beside the coals of what he figured had been Yancey's camp. He felt of them and they were still warm. Standing up, he slowly studied the area. A dark spot on the ground just a few feet from him drew his attention. Two quick strides and he was kneeling beside the spot. Picking up the sand the spot had darkened, he smelled it. 'Blood', he thought to himself. Standing back up he walked the perimeter of the camp but found nothing else. He made a bigger circle around the camp this time and found what he was looking for that confirmed what he thought. A bloody shirt was lying beside a cactus and he was sure it belonged to the man that was wounded. McClellan and the patrol arrived at that time.

"Over here, Captain."

"Was this their camp?" McClellan asked

"I'm sure of it," Tye said. "Here's a bloody shirt I found in the bushes." He handed the bloody shirt to McClellan who looked at it and nodded his agreement. He tossed the shirt back on the ground.

"How far behind them?"

"From the warmth of the coals and the horse manure where they picketed the horses, I'd say no more than two hours."

"Tracks?"

"Over there," Tye answered nodding to where his saw the tracks leading away from the camp. "They're heading deeper into the hills."

"Why do you suppose they're going in that direction?"

"Homesteads. The bastards figure there are several homesteads in the hills. They need food and other supplies, like ammunition. If I know Yancey, he'll kill everyone at every homestead. He's bad, Captain. I've brought in some bad men before but Yancey's different. He will kill just to watch the expression on his victims faces as they die. He'll rape the women and young girls and then cut their throats."

31

Tye felt the bile coming up in his throat thinking of this man. He never knew the feeling of pure hate before but he could not deny the feeling now. The thought of his wife being threatened by this piece of trash filled him with a rage he never felt before. "He needs to be in hell, Captain. I aim to send him there. No waiting for a trial this time, I'm gonna kill him." Tye jumped on Sandy and headed west. He looked back over his shoulder. "You coming?"

McClellan was frozen like a statue. He had just seen a side of Tye he never saw before and it scared the hell out of him. He would never forget the apathetic look on the scout's face as he uttered those last words.

"CAPTAIN," Norwood shouted. "We need to go." The sound of the sergeant's voice brought him out of his trance. He mounted his horse and not saying a word, headed out. Tye was barely in sight as Norwood pulled up beside McClellan.

"Everything okay, Sir?"

"I...I guess so." Norwood was sure Tye said something that had affected McClellan. He pressed the issue.

"If I may ask, Sir, what did Tye say that's bothering you?'

McClellan looked at Norwood. "He said that he wasn't going to bring Yancey in so he could wait for a trial and hanging. He's gonna kill him."

"Tye said that?" McClellan nodded.

"I believe him too. I will never forget that look on his face when he said it."

"Tye tell you about the homesteaders in the area up ahead?"

"Yes. He said that's why Yancey was headed there."

"Tye has some friends up in those hills. I'm sure he's worried about them and frustrated that he is pretty much helpless to stop it. By the time we catch up, it will be too late for some. As far as him killing that piece of shit, I won't lose a minute's sleep over it. I hope he does and makes it as slow and painful as possible. Think about it, Sir. No telling how many men, women, and even children that man has killed. He's gonna answer for those sins before God and Tye is just going to help him get there." He pulled his mount up and then fell in behind McClellan's mount.

McClellan mulled over what Tye and Norwood had said. 'Maybe they're right,' he thought. 'This land has no law except the army and a few men like Tye to try and control the vermin that's here. For most out here the gun is the law and most of the time, justice is swift. Maybe in a few years, things will change.'

Tye was thinking about his friends in the hills and unconsciously picked up the pace. His senses were on razor edge, watching for trouble and following tracks at the same time, tended to keep a man a little busy. He knew a bullet could come at any second and it made the adrenalin flow through his veins, making him even more aware of every thing going on around him. Not only was he watching the terrain but he was watching Sandy too. A horse can see and smell better than a man and could save a man's life if he paid attention to a sudden snort, stomping of the feet, or their ears twitching. His bacon had been saved a couple of times by paying attention to Sandy.

Out here on scout, away from the fort, away from town, Tye felt free. He loved the feel of the wind on his face, the heat of the sun on his back, and open land that seemed to have no end. The land ahead was becoming rugged, with many arroyos and folds in the land where a man could hide, waiting to ambush his victim. By the same token, the deep cuts and hills made it easier for a man to remain unseen and Tye was a master at remaining invisible.

He suddenly pulled Sandy up, dismounted and picked up a stick. He stuck the stick into the horse droppings, pulled it out and looked at the matter on the stick. He immediately dropped to one knee, throwing the stick down and cocking his Sharps. The texture of the manure told him he was only minutes behind the men, close enough to be damn careful. He knew they were not stupid enough to believe they were not being pursued. He remembered the last words Yancey had yelled at him, "The next time I lay eyes on you, you are a dead man."

He studied every rock and bush all around him, then searched farther out. Satisfied there was no immediate danger, he stood up and decided to wait on the patrol. He took out the makings and rolled himself a smoke. He inhaled deeply and looked up at the blue, cloudless sky and blew a perfect ring of smoke. There was no breeze and the rings seemed to have a life of their own. The rings floated in one direction as they rose into the air and then in another direction. 'Smoke's just like I used to be, Sandy, free and drifting in no particular direction. Rebecca changed all that.' He smiled. His thoughts were interrupted by McClellan and the patrol arriving.

"Are we gaining on them?" McClellan asked.

"Close enough to be damn careful."

"Sergeant, Norwood," the captain called out.

"Here, Sir."

"Have the men on alert. Tye thinks we are close to the men we are after. Tell the men it will be hell to pay if I catch one of them dozing in the saddle."

"Yes Sir." Norwood said turning his mount around and repeating the order word for word. The men immediately sit up straighter in the saddle, a couple of the men smiled at Norwood and he smiled back, shaking his head. He thought the order wasn't necessary as most of these men were veterans of many a patrol and all were battle tested.

Norwood was a career man but knew he would never be more than what he was, a First Sergeant, maybe a Sergeant Major. He had been in the service since before the War and at Clark since the fort had been regarrisoned in '66. He was born in West Virginia. His parents worked themselves to death on a small farm and he swore he would never push a plow again. He was nineteen when he joined the Union Army in '59. He was given a field commission in '63 but, as so many others, was busted back when the War ended. He was young for a sergeant, but he was tougher than nails. Despite his age, he was respected by the enlisted men, even the older ones. They knew that he could be counted on when things got tight and if they stuck close to him, they just might see another sunrise.

~~~

The McIntosh family's homestead was fifteen miles north of Brackett. The home was located in a small valley and only a stones throw from a creek. They had good grass and plenty of water for their stock which included fifteen goats, five head of cattle with four calves, a bull, and six horses. They also had several chickens that kept them in eggs. Living in the house was William, his wife, Joanna, and their nineteen year old twin boys, William Jr., and Luke.

They had homesteaded here eight years ago, having moved all their belongings from their home in Alabama. They had moved before the War. William Sr. had seen the trouble coming long before, and wanted to get out before the fighting began. They never had slaves and didn't want any. He also didn't want his sons fighting in the war and he knew the young men would be conscripted into the army.

They loved the valley from the first moment they lay eyes on it. It was a half mile wide and ran east and west. They built their home on the north side, at the base of the cliffs that formed the wall of the canyon. The south wall was not cliffs, but a steep sloping hill. The north wind in the winter was kept from them by the cliffs behind them and during the summer, the west and southwest winds blowing down the valley helped with the heat.

They had been bothered only once by Apaches and a couple of times by men too lazy to work and wanting handouts. Back in Alabama, William had been known to win a lot of shooting contest. The Apache learned of this the hard way as he had killed four of them when they attacked his home about three years ago. They hadn't bothered him since. Even so, William and his sons were never too far from their rifles and each wore a sidearm. The boys were good shots too but their skill fell a little short of their pa.

They were a very happy family, content to live their lives where they were and not bother anyone else. Tye had come by three or four times in the last two years when on scout and on a couple occasions, had eaten dinner with them. They considered Tye their friend and he was always welcome. They, like most of the homesteaders, knew what Tye and the army had done for them and they were appreciative. The two boys were always asking Tye questions about what he did and if they might do it when they were old enough. Tye had laughed and told them to get married and find a safer occupation, like their pa had done... and be home every night.

Tye hadn't seen them since he and Rebecca had gotten married. The McIntosh family had come to Fort Clark for the wedding as did most other folks within twenty or so miles of Clark. This was typical of any celebration. There weren't many opportunities to have a party in this country and folks just wouldn't miss an opportunity to get together. The men would visit and catch up on the latest news, the women would catch up on the gossip, and the children, who seldom were around kids their own age, could get acquainted and play games. If the folks had the opportunity, they would have a dance as everyone in this country loved dancing. The wedding of Tye and Rebecca had been the last big shindig that just about everyone within a thirty mile radius of Clark had gotten together.

~~~

Yancey and the men with him had picked up the pace. They had seen the small cloud of dust behind them and figured it to be the patrol. Now deep in the hills they felt a little safer. The ground was rocky and the horses were leaving little notice of their passing. They were bunched tightly together when they rounded around a large clump of cedars and got the shock of their lives.

Sitting on their horses were three men, guns leveled at Yancey and his men.

"Don't reckon any of you gents feel lucky enough to go for his gun," the man in the middle said. He was a big man, wide square shoulders, long black hair that touched his shoulders and deep blue eyes. His face was covered with a black beard and a wad of tobacco pushed his cheek out. He looked like the two men with him, dirty and sweaty. He spit a stream of the black stuff and it splattered on a flat rock.

"Come on out boys," he said, "and join the party."

"James…James Mason? Is that you?" Tom asked the man who had been doing the talking. It drew quick looks from all the men. Four other men came out of the brush, weapons drawn. Yancey was glad he hadn't pulled his gun and tried to shoot his way out.

The man Tom had called out kicked his mount in the flanks and moved a few steps closer.

"I'll be damned…Tom. What are you doing out here?" he asked putting his gun back in the holster; and motioning the others to do the same. A sigh of relieve came from Yancey, Grant, and Mitch. All of them had figured they were dead men. A second look at these men, their dirty clothes, unwashed bearded faces, feathers sticking out of their hats, and twin bandoleers full of ammunition crossing their chests gave away their occupation, Comancheros.

Tom and the man he had called James shook hands.

"What are you doing out here?" the man asked Tom again. Tom looked back over his shoulder and then back at James.

"Patrol is after us."

"THE ARMY," he exclaimed loudly. "What did you do to get them after you?"

"Busted this man here out of the guard house at Clark," he answered as he put his hand on Yancey's Shoulder. "James, this is Yancey Cates." James jerked his head and stared at the man James said was Cates.

"That true...you Cates?"

"Been my handle as long as I can remember," Yancey replied.

"Heard about you. You're supposed to be a bad-ass."

"Yancey sat up a little straighter in the saddle. "That's the word that's out." The man looked back at Tom.

"That patrol wouldn't have a scout by the name of Watkins scouting for it?" he asked. Yancey figured he was fixing to hear the same shit again about this great man...God...or whatever the hell he was. He was surprised by the man's reply after Tom said Watkins was scouting for the patrol.

"You boys hear that?" James asked his men. "Looks like we may have another chance at that sonofabitch."

"What's he done to put a burr in your butt?" Yancey asked.

"Not much," James said. "About a year ago, my brother and some men were down here calling on some homesteaders. Wasn't doing much you know, just robbing, raping, and killing," he said in a voice showing no emotion. "Watkins led a patrol that ran them down, killed all but two, my brother and a man named Leroy. They were hung in Brackett."

"I thought you boys were way north of here, trading with the Comanche."

"Were," James answered, "but the Rangers and the army are cracking down on us boys. Thought we would come south and see what's down here. Lucky I recognized you, are all of you boys would be buzzard bait by now. We were aiming to kill all of you and take whatever money and guns you had...and your horses."

"Maybe we can join up," Yancey said. "I'm gonna kill that damn scout after I kill a few of these Yankee loving homesteaders. We can split whatever we can take." James looked at his men. They just shrugged their shoulders.

James reached out and shook Yancey's hand. "Howdy partner," he said laughing.

37

~~~

"Damn and double damn," Tye muttered under his breath. He was watching the meeting through binoculars while hiding behind some cedar about a hundred yards away. He knew that he had a real problem now. "Comancheros... it has to be Comancheros." He watched the men shake hands and ride off together. He stood up and walked back to Sandy. He stuck his left foot in the stirrup, swung his other leg over and settled in the saddle to wait on McClellan, Garrison, and the patrol.

Chapter Five

"Seen you on top of the hill. Did you see them?" McClellan asked before he even got to Tye. Tye waited until he got close before answering.

"Yeah, I saw them."

"Well then, let's get this over with." He turned in the saddle and started to give the order to move out.

"Wait just a damn minute, Captain," Tye said grabbing the captain's horse's reins. "We have a problem."

"What do you mean by that?"

"Comancheros, Captain."

"What does that mean?" Lieutenant Garrison asked.

"Yancey and the men with him just met and joined up with seven or eight men who from the looks of them, they are Comancheros."

"I don't understand. What are the Comancheros?"

"Comancheros are the scum of the earth, Lieutenant. They kill, rob, and rape. They also kidnap young girls to work in whore houses or sell them as slaves in Mexico. They trade with the Comanche, giving them whiskey, guns, and trinkets. Their guns have killed no telling how many settlers and soldiers. Like I said, they are bad news, almost as bad as Yancey. You put the two together and you have a real dangerous situation, especially since they know we are coming behind them. Things are gonna get real bloody from here on."

"SERGEANT FINNEY," McClellan shouted.

"Here, Sir," Finney said coming up behind McClellan.

"Tye and Dan say Yancey and his group have joined forces with eight or so Comancheros."

"COMANCHEROS," Finney shouted. "Shit. What the hell they doing down here. They're usually a couple hundred or so miles north."

"Dunno," McClellan answered, "but Tye thinks that's who they are." McClellan looked at Finney and Garrison, then at Tye and Dan.

"This changes things men. They now have as many men as we have so we can't just go charging in when we find them."

"That's right, Captain," Dan said. "It's different now. We have twelve or so men that will hang if brought in. I don't think they will give up and they sure as hell ain't going to die easy."

"Dan's right, Sir" Tye said. "I think maybe you should consider sending a dispatch to Thurston explaining the situation. Not only do they have as many men as we do, I bet next months pay that they have repeating rifles."

McClellan looked at Tye. "Why do you think that?"

"Comancheros don't trade old single shots, Sir. They probably have the thirteen shot Henrys."

McClellan looked away, staring at the horizon, starring but not really seeing anything as his mind raced.   It had not occurred to him they might have the Henry's. He looked at the ground, scratching his forehead. "I'll send the dispatch." He took a pad out of his pants pocket and a pencil from his shirt pocket.

> *Major Thurston*
> *We have killed one of the men and wounded another but we have a problem. Yancey and the others have joined with eight or so men we believe to be Comancheros. They now have eleven or twelve men and Tye thinks there is a good chance they have repeating rifles. If true, our number of men and our firepower is dangerously less than theirs. We are continuing our pursuit. If possible send another patrol. Private Hunt can show them the way back here and then pick up our trail.*
> *Captain McClellan*

When finished, McClellan told Sergeant Norwood to give the dispatch to Hunt to deliver to Thurston.

"We going on or not?" he asked Tye.

"Yes Sir, we are," Tye answered sarcastically riding away. "You coming or staying Dan?" Dan mounted up and galloped away to catch up. When he did, he pulled along beside Tye.

"Known you a long time, Tye; never saw you this worked up. I know that you have friends in these hills and I know that sonofabitch said he was gonna get Rebecca, then you. But you know what could happen if you go off half-cocked. You could get yourself killed and that's sure as hell not going to help Rebecca none. I know you are anxious to catch him. I know you are gonna kill the bastard but going storming down the trail could get you, not him, killed. About four years ago, my oldest brother's wife was raped by some Mexicans. He swore he'd kill every one of them and stormed into the hills to do it. He never came back. She got raped and lost her husband too. She killed herself shortly thereafter. What I'm trying to say, Tye, is slow down and think things out and don't leave Rebecca a widow. She is in good hands at the fort with Buff and Thurston, so just concentrate on locating Yancey and the others and then see how things play out. You can't take them all by yourself."

Tye reined Sandy up. He put his hands on the pommel of his saddle and took a deep breath and then let it out slowly. He looked over at his friend and smiled. "You're a good friend, Dan. What you just said makes a hell of a lot of sense and I needed to hear it." He placed his hand on Dan's shoulder. "Let's get busy earning our pay and find those bastards. You track and old Sandy and I will watch for trouble." They headed out. Tye looked over his shoulder to make sure the patrol was following. The two hours left of daylight was spent tracking, watching for trouble. They were less than an hour behind the men and both were expecting trouble any second.

Dan said. "Let's wait on McClellan, Tye."

"I was thinking the same thing," Tye replied. "We're only minutes from full dark and it would be suicide to keep going. You wait here for the patrol and I'll find a place to camp." Dan dismounted, sat on his haunches holding his horse's reins to wait. Tye left the trail looking for a place to camp.

~~~

A couple miles farther into the hills, Yancey and his group were making camp.

"No fire," Yancey remarked. "I guarantee you that damn scout is close behind us. Hell, he may be watching us now." Most of the men started looking around. Yancey laughed. "He ain't no damn ghost or God, he's a man like you and me, bleeds like you and me."

41

"Never said he was anything but a man," Mason said. "But he's one hell of one…mucho hombre as the Mexicans would say. Old Billy there could attest to that. Right Billy?" Yancy's eyes went to the man called Billy. He was one rough looking sonofabitch: thick through the shoulders and chest and his arms looked like a blacksmith's. His face, what he could see that wasn't covered by his thick beard, was dark, like an Indian's. His eyes were menacing. The man definitely had the looks of one you would not want to mess with.

"Bout a year ago," the man named Billy said, "I was in Brackett in one of the saloons. Had me one too many and started tearing up the place. Heard a voice behind me saying 'that's enough; now turn slowly around with your hands empty.' I did, expecting to see a man with a gun pointed at me. Instead, it was this man standing there, arms hanging loosely at his side, fist clinched. I stepped into him and the fight was on. Only trouble, I never landed a blow and he beat the living hell out of me. Only time I can remember that happening."

"He's a tough sonofabitch, I'll admit that," Yancey said. "Beat the hell out of me once or twice too."

"I'm thinking maybe we should send someone back and see how many are coming," Mason said.

Yancey nodded. "Good idea."

"Jason, you and Matt take a look see." The two men started to mount their horses. "Walk," Mason said. "Damn noise the horses make will get you caught or killed." Both men nodded and took off down their back trail.

Moving quickly and quietly, they had covered about a mile when they stopped to catch their breath and listen. Kneeling down, they listened for any unusual sounds. They heard nothing but the breeze rustling the leaves of the mesquite. They stayed there about five minutes, saying nothing, just listening.

"Let's go," Matt whispered. Standing up, the two men moved toward where they figured the soldiers were, moving very carefully and without a sound. Five minutes later, they stopped as the slight breeze in their face brought the sound of men talking. Down on their bellies, they crawled toward the sound. After five minutes of crawling, the voices were much louder. Stopping, Matt put his finger to his lips to signal Jason not to say anything. Looking through the sage, they could see the small fire and several soldiers sitting around it. The raucous laughter meant they were probably telling some 'war' stories that took place in the rooms above the saloons in Brackett. They could barely make out the officers who were standing away from the men. They were talking with two men who appeared to be scouts. One of them was very tall and thick through the shoulders and chest.

"We're close Captain, real close to them," Tye said. "It would be smart to put out the fire and double the guards. Either Dan or me will be awake also. They know we are behind them so we need to expect trouble."

"I agree," McClellan replied. "Lieutenant, would you set the sentries and see that the fire is put out."

"Right away Sir."

McClellan asked. "Do you think they would hit us at night?"

"I sure as hell would if I was in their shoes." Dan answered. Tye nodded in agreement.

"We need to be ready, Captain."

"What do you suggest?" Tye looked in all directions outside the firelight. He nodded his head. "Over there, Captain." They, McClellan, Dan, and Tye walked away from the men and farther away from where the two outlaws lay. Tye sat down on a rock and indicated to McClellan and Dan to do the same.

"Have the same feeling I have, Tye?" Dan asked. Tye nodded. Very quietly, Tye said, "Captain, can you call Garrison and Norwood over here?"

"Lieutenant Garrison. Sergeant Norwood. Would you please come over here?" Both were there in a couple of seconds.

"Fire's out and sentry schedule is set, Captain," Norwood said.

"Good. Now listen up. Tye and Dan think we are in for trouble, possibly tonight. We have all seen before these feelings they have pan out, so I think we had better listen to what they think."

"First off, don't look around because of what I'm fixing to say," Tye whispered. "I think we have company close by. Haven't seen or heard them, but both Dan and me had that strange feeling of being watched. I know that sounds funny but you have heard that some men can feel it when someone is staring at them. It's true. It's happened to me more than once and to Dan also. It has saved our butts more than once. It has not been true all the time, but enough times to be careful." He kneeled down and so did everyone else. Picking up a stick he put an 'x' on the

43

ground. He drew a line close to one side. "This 'x' is our camp and this line is that arroyo that is right behind us. Forget about trouble coming from that direction. It would be impossible to sneak up on a deaf man that way with the rocks and steep sides." He paused for a couple seconds and looked around, and then using the stick he drew two arrows, the tips pointing at the camp.

"If they come it will be from one of these two directions."

"I can see why they would not come by way of the arroyo but that leaves three sides. Why do you think they won't attack from the direction that you don't have an arrow by?" McClellan asked.

Dan spoke up before Tye could answer. "Did you notice the landscape in that direction before it became dark?'

"I don't guess I paid much attention."

"Remember I told you once that it was the little things out here that one forgets or doesn't pay attention to that gets him killed.

"I remember," McClellan replied.

"This is one of those things that can help us. The reason they won't attack from that direction is cactus, Captain. A hell of a lot of cactus. It's so thick a man would have a hard time getting thru it in the daytime. It would be impossible at night. When you are on patrol, Captain, always make sure you or your scout picks a spot to camp that can be defended fairly easy. It ain't always possible, but do it when it is."

"I'll remember."

"Me too," Garrison chimed in.

"If they are coming, it will be early, just before daylight. That is when the last watch will be most susceptible to being careless. I suggest we all get some shuteye while we can. We need to roll out of the bedrolls about three a.m. and get our defenses set up. Have the men hit the sack with their guns close by in case they come early...if they come."

The temperature had dropped considerably since the sun had dropped behind the hills. It was probably eighty degrees at mid day and now was in the mid fifties. It made for good sleeping. Everyone except the sentries were snug in their bedrolls...trying to find sleep. Most were finding it hard to come by. Being told that before daylight, you may be fighting for your life was a little unsettling. Tye was in his bedroll as Dan took the first turn at watching for trouble.

Dan was making sure the sentries were alert. The little breeze there was came from the southwest which was not good. The breeze would be blowing into the bandits face and away from the camp. Any sound made by the men would be carried away from the soldiers. Dan made sure the guards understood that fact and kept their eyes away from the camp and into the darkness. They were a group of nervous soldiers and the eerie sound of a coyote's howling didn't help matters any.

~~~

Jason and Matt had made their way back to the bandits' camp. Mason and Yancey both were anxious to hear what they had found.

"Did you see them?" Mason asked.

"Yeah, we found their camp," Jason answered.

"There's nine or ten soldiers and two scouts," Matt added.

"Watkins?" Yancey questioned.

"Watkins is there. At least we think it was him." Jason said. "Big man, maybe six-two or so, thick chest and arms; wore blue cavalry pants, Apache boots, and buckskin shirt."

"That's the bastard," Yancey said as he stood up and faced the men.

"What's the plan?" Billy asked.

"We'll hit them about five a.m., an hour or so before daylight. With these repeaters and the element of surprise we should have a big advantage. Now get some shuteye."

"Why don't we just keep moving and stay ahead of them?" Mitch asked.

"Because we have an opportunity to surprise them and if not kill them, maybe at least discourage them some."

~~~

Back at the fort at the O'Malley's home, Rebecca and the O'Malley's were being entertained by Buff and his stories of the shining times. At Sergeant O'Malley's request, he told of the first years he spent trapping, before he met Ben. He wanted Buff to save the stories of his times with Ben for Tye to hear. Buff was more than willing to talk.

45

"Started trappin beever in '16. I wus sorta like Ben wus when I met him, greener than anee wun in tha montons." He chuckled to himself. "Not more greener than tha lootenant Garrison though." He and everyone laughed remembering Buff's good natured kidding the Lieutenant when they first met about how green he was. That thar ferst yeer wus tuff. I damned neer starv'd to deth then I damn neer froze ta deth. Had very few plews tha ferst yeer at tha rondovue. Tha's whare I met Bridger and Stumpee. Tha wurn't ferst class trapp'rs as of yet so we sorter learned tagether over tha next few yeers.

Tha second yeer wus a little better. We all had a bett'r understanding whut we faced and we wur bett'r prepared fur it. Tha onliest truble we had wur Grizz tha second yeer. We musta killed half aduzen or so. We had us sum close calls tha yeer with them. Stumpee pruved he wus a man who kud be depended on. Bridger wus in a fix wunce tha yeer. Got hisself treed by a old moma tha had sum yung cubs. She had Bridger's rifle and pistol balls in her and she was mor'n upset. Tha tree Bridger got hisself in wusn't a big tree and tha old she grizz wus about ta knok him out uf it by shakin it sumthang feerce. Old Stumpee kame runnin and shot tha bear again with his rifle. Tha old bear tuk off after him." Buff laughed. "Funniest damn thang I ever did see. Stumpee, with them thar long skinnee legs jus a pumping, arms flaing, runnin jus as fas as he kud. Tha she bear, wal she wus closing fast on him. I wus a gud distance away but I fired aneeway and hit her and she went down hard. Thou't it wus over, but she got up an charged old Stumpee again. Stump wusn't runnin. He pulled his pistol and shot the grizz between the eyes. She rared up on them hind legs and luked 10 fut tall.

Stumpee pulled his Bowie out an wuz fixin to die fiteing. Like I sade, she was rared up fixin ta pounce on Stumpee when all uf a sudden she jus kolasped, rite on top of Stumpee, deader than a peece of wud. When she fell, Stumpee buried tha Bowie in tha she bear's chest. We ran to him and it tuk all me an Bridger had to git that bear offin him. He wus busted up sum, brused ribs and hurt sholder, but happier than hell. Sade he dun killed a grizz with his knife. We just kud not tale him tha bear wus already dead. He tol tha store fur years at tha rondavus and me an Bridger always sade it wus tru."

Buff leaned back in his chair and laughed again. "Stump sade he wus gonna kill tha old bear with his knife, wusn't runnin no mo. Wal, both Bridger and me knu better. He wus just plum winded, kudn't run another step. Aneeway, he sav'd old Bridger tha day and pruv'd ta everwun he wus a man ta ride tha riv'r with."

"That's quite a story, Buff," Sergeant O'Malley said, "and a good way to end the evening. I need to check on the sentries, make sure they are where they are supposed to be. Let me walk you two home."

"Thank you two for a wonderful evening," Rebecca said as she got up from her chair. "I'll see you in the morning," she said, hugging Mrs. O'Malley.

Gary McMillan

Chapter Six

The rain started as a light mist while Tye was on watch and continued when he was relieved by Dan around two a.m... He fell asleep immediately, snug in his bedroll, his hat over his face to keep the mist off. The coolness of the early morning and the patter of the rain helped him fall into a deep, relaxing sleep. The rain, falling a little harder now would make the landscape look a little different in the morning with all the white dust washed off the short brown grass and the leaves of the mesquite and sage. There was no sound other than the snores of sleeping men and the footfalls of the sentries.

Tye suddenly awoke with a start, fully awake. He raised himself up slowly, ears alert for any sound and his eyes sweeping the camp. Hearing and seeing nothing unusual, he stood up and looked around again. He saw Dan coming toward him, moving quick and in a crouch.

"They're out there, Tye. I just heard a loud snap, probably a mesquite limb being stepped on," Dan whispered. Tye knew that's what woke him up. Even in a sound sleep, a man had better be tuned in to the night sounds if he wanted to survive out here. Any noise out of the ordinary should alert him to possible trouble.

"Wake up McClellan and Garrison and have them come over here." Less than a minute both men, along with Dan, were crouched down by Tye. "Dan and me both heard a noise a couple minutes ago, probably a mesquite limb that was stepped on and snapped."

"Could have been an animal, maybe a deer or other large animal," Garrison stated.

"Could be, but it wasn't," Dan said.

"This time of the morning and with the rain, the animals are holed up...except the two legged ones. I think we had better wake the men up and find a defensive position for each one," Tye suggested.

"Get the men up and over here," McClellan said, speaking to Garrison.

"Yes Sir." He moved away from them, toward the sleeping men. In less than two minutes the men were assembled around Tye and Dan. Garrison had made sure each had his weapon with him.

~~~

Yancey jerked his head around trying to see who had stepped on the limb. He knew that sound had carried to the camp and if they didn't attack now, the camp may be ready for them. Mason was beside him.

"Do you think they heard that?" he asked.

"Stupid Yankee soldiers probably didn't, but you can bet your ass one or both of those scouts did."

"What's your suggestion we do?"

"Spread the men out and let's hit them hard with everything we have. The seven Henry's we have with their thirteen shot magazine should be more than enough firepower. Let's get it done."

Mason turned to the man next to him and whispered, "Spread out and get ready to attack the camp. Pass the word."

~~~

"We are fixing to be hit and hit hard," Tye told the men quietly. "Spread out and find some cover. The attack should come from that direction over..." he didn't finish as what sounded like fifty guns began firing at them.

"TAKE COVER," McClellan shouted, his voice barely heard over the noise of the guns. A second later he was hit and fell to the ground. Tye and Dan had dropped to the ground and scooted to the right. Garrison, and the men who had not been slow in hitting the wet ground, moved to the left. Three men, who were slow to react, were down. The rest could hear the men crashing through the brush, racing toward the camp.

"WAIT TILL I GIVE THE ORDER TO FIRE," Garrison ordered. The men were about thirty yards away when they let loose another volley into the camp.

"FIRE," Garrison ordered. The soldiers fired the single shot Sharps and then grabbed their Navy Colts and fired them. Several of the attacking men went down. The effectiveness of the soldiers' fire stopped the attack as the attackers hit the ground, at least the ones that were not sprawled on the wet ground, dead. Both sides were firing now. They could not see each other but were firing at the muzzle flashes. Tye and Dan were firing and then moving before firing again, not staying in one place more than a few seconds.

"Let's retreat and fight another day," Mason said to Yancey.

"They were ready for us," Yancey said. "If I knew who the sonofabitch was that stepped on that branch, I'd kill him." They started scooting backwards, stopping periodically to fire their guns. The others that were not hit were doing the same. Both the outlaws and the soldiers were firing with fairly good accuracy, considering the darkness and the rain. The 'thump' of bullets hitting flesh could be heard followed by grunts of those hit. Finally the outlaws stood up and raced away from the camp. Tye and Dan were up and moving after them, as well as Garrison and a couple of the soldiers. Running, stopping, firing, running again; after a couple hundred yards of this, they stopped and headed back to camp to see how much damage had been done.

"Norwood, get me a causality report." Garrison ordered.

"YO," Norwood answered. Garrison met Dan and Tye at the unconscious body of McClellan. Tye kneeled and rolled the captain over on his back. McClellan groaned.

"Damn," Tye said disgustingly. He saw the hole high in McClellan's chest, close to the shoulder, probably in a lung. McClellan coughed and a bloody froth bubbled out between his lips. Norwood came back.

"I have the report, Sir."

"Let's have it."

"Three dead and four with slight wounds plus the captain. Two of the wounded can continue. The other two need medical attention."

"Thank you, Sergeant. Tend to the wounded if you will."

"Yes Sir." Norwood replied. "How is the captain?"

"Not good," Garrison said as he kneeled and opened the captain's tunic pressing a kerchief on the wound, stemming the flow of blood somewhat. "What do you think, Tye?"

"He'll never make it if he doesn't get medical help and quick." They walked to where the bodies were laid out.

Norwood looked up. "Corporal Phillips, Private Lightfoot, and Private Hill, are dead, Sir."

"I'm going to have to send a man back with the dead and with McClellan and the other two wounded men," Garrison said. Tye nodded.

"Dan and me will make a travois for the Captain to lie on."

"How far are we from Clark, Tye?" Garrison asked.

"If they leave quickly, they should be there by late afternoon."

"Do you think McClellan will make it?"

"I believe he will if he gets medical attention in the next few hours. The bullet went clean thru which is good. Dan, get me a bottle of whiskey from your saddlebag." When Dan returned he handed the bottle to Tye. Pulling the cork from the bottle, he poured some into the hole in the chest. McClellan groaned but remained unconscious. It was repeated on the exit hole and then bandaged with cloth from a clean shirt found in McClellan's saddle bag.

"Corporal Phipps," Garrison said.

"Yes Sir."

"Can you find Fort Clark?"

"Yes Sir. I can"

"Good. Get the dead on their mounts, and take them and the captain directly there as fast as you can." Garrison turned to Norwood. "Take Private Garcia as soon as it is light enough and see how many of the outlaws are dead."

"Will do, Sir. And if any are wounded?" Garrison did not answer, just looked at him.

"Yes Sir." Norwood said understanding what the silence meant. The Lieutenant did not want any burden of more wounded...he just could not give the order.

Phipps had the dead tied to their mounts and McClellan on a travois behind his horse. He saluted the Lieutenant and was on his way to Fort Clark. A shot startled both Tye and Garrison. They both turned to see Norwood putting his pistol back in his holster. A minute later he reported four dead outlaws. "Found these, Sir." He handed two, thirteen shot Henry repeating rifles and a bandoleer full of shells to Garrison.

Garrison laid one of the rifles on the ground, holding the other, turning it over in his hands, inspecting it. Tye picked up the other and looked it over. He worked the lever several times, ejecting shells each time.

"God in Heaven," Private Hunt declared. "What the army could do with them."

"You don't have to worry none about that, Private," Tye said. "The army takes changes very slowly. It will be a few years before they change, right Lieutenant?"

"Seems so," Garrison muttered still admiring the Henry. "You take one, Tye, and Dan you the other. You have what were in the rifles plus about forty or so rounds on the belt."

"You sure, Lieutenant?" Tye asked.

"I'm sure. Go over there and shoot them...see how they work and get used to them while we get things together here."

Tye and Dan walked a few yards away. Dan emptied his rifle as Tye had done. They shoved three shells into the slot on the side of the chamber. Tye walked off fifty yards and put one of the dead outlaws hat on top of a cactus. He stepped back and hollered at Dan to hit it. Dan took aim, let his breath out slowly and squeezed the trigger. The rifle bucked against his shoulder and the hat was blown off the cactus. He levered another shell and hit the hat again while it lay on the ground. "DAMN," He uttered under his breath. Tye came back.

"What do you think?"

"Shoots true and the recoil is not as bad as the Sharps. Damn nice gun, Tye."

"Walk out there about seventy-five yards and hang the hat up," Tye said. While Dan was walking away, he jerked the rifle to his shoulder, and sighted at an imaginary target. The gun felt good in his hands, like it belonged there. He lowered it and pushed three shells into the slot. Dan had placed the hat about seventy-five yards away and stepped aside. Tye sighted down the barrel, let his breath out and squeezed the trigger slowly. The hammer fell and the gun roared. The hat disappeared. Tye fired the other two shells as fast as he could work the lever. He lowered the gun and looked at it, admiring it even more than he did a few minutes ago. "Sweet," he muttered.

Dan arrived about that time and laughed when he heard Tye mutter. "Damn and double damn." They loaded the rifles and walked back to camp.

"Well?" Garrison said.

"Sweet, Lieutenant. Real sweet," Tye said. "We ready to move out?"

"We're ready."

"Sir," Norwood said. "Phipps is coming back." All heads turned toward the sound of the horses coming toward them. Arriving, Phipps dismounted.

"The Captain came around and wanted to speak to you, Sir." Garrison, Tye, and

Dan walked around to the travois where McClellan lay. Squatting on their heels, they looked at McClellan, waiting for him to speak. McClellan slowly raised his hand and placed it on Garrison's shoulder; spoke to him in a low, cracking voice that made every word spoken laborious.

"Ho…How many were…killed?"

"Three, Sir."

"Th…three? Who?"

"Corporal Phillips, Private Lightfoot and Private Hill, Sir."

"God." McClellan muttered, letting his head fall back on the folded up tunic that served as a pillow. He turned his head toward Garrison and with a whispered voice. "Don't le…" he didn't finish, losing consciousness. His arm fell limply to the ground.

In a hushed tone, Garrison asked, "Is…is he gone?"

"He's lost a lot of blood, Lieutenant," Dan said. "Sleep is the best thing for him right now." Dan picked up the captain's arm that was dangling off the travois and lay it across his chest.

"Phipps, get the captain and the rest to the fort straight-a-way. No stopping."

"Yes Sir." He turned and remounting his horse, was soon out of sight.

"Let's get after the rest of them then," Tye said. He and Dan loped their horses out in front, then slowed to a walk. Both men felt a new confidence, more security than either had known before, not that they needed it. They were always confident in their abilities but having the ability to fire twenty-six shots as fast as they could have fired four to six between them before helped one feel that way.

Garrison didn't bother to ask about burying the dead outlaws. He knew Tye's thoughts on that from the previous patrol that brought in Yancey. "Leave them for the buzzards," Tye had said. "If you really knew just what type of men these were, you wouldn't even give burying them a thought." He led what was left of the patrol, following the scouts.

"Been intending to ask; why do you suppose they attacked us instead of getting farther away?" Dan asked.

Tye gripped the pommel on his saddle with both hands, head bowed, lips pursed in thought. It was a few seconds before he spoke. "I think they thought they could surprise us, maybe kill most of us with their superior firepower. Maybe they were going to try and discourage us; maybe just because of simple hate of the Union Army. Yancey, hell he just likes to see people die. Might have succeeded if not for that snapped limb one of them stepped on." He looked back at the patrol, what was left of it. "I really don't know why, just a bunch of theories."

Gary McMillan

Chapter Seven

Yancey, Mason and the remaining members of the group had not let up the fast pace since the fight a couple hours ago. Yancey finally reined in as did the men behind him. Mason pulled his mount up alongside Yancey's.

"Been doing some thinking, Yancey."

"About our attacking the blue-belly camp?"

"Yeah. I think we let our hate get the best of us...probably should not have done that. It cost us some good men."

Yancey walked his horse a ways before speaking. "Probably...but I don't think there would be a Yankee problem if they had not received a few seconds warning by the sonofabitch that stepped on that limb. We'd had them in their bedrolls."

"Don't know Yancey. They sure were quick to react, almost like they were ready...like they knew we were coming." Yancey had thought the same thing but would not admit it. He'd rather blame the disaster on someone else...who ever snapped that limb. He'd thought that maybe that damn scout had somehow known they were coming. He didn't want to believe that either. Men just didn't have the ability to feel trouble coming he thought. "Well, how many did we lose?" he asked in a tone that made Mason feel that he didn't give a damn.

"Four dead and one wounded. Lewis, Calvin, Billy, and Jason are dead and Clint is hit in the shoulder."

"Is he gonna be able to stay up?"

Mason looked at him, not believing anyone could be so cold. He thought the man could at least go talk to Clint, ask if he was okay. He was getting an uneasy feeling about Yancey...a damn uneasy feeling. He had rode with the worse men one could imagine but from what he had seen and heard about Yancey, the man sent a cold chill up his spine. He was getting away from him the first chance he got. He figured Yancey was the devil reincarnated and he was a dead man if he stayed with him. Since he had joined up with Yancey and his men,

57

three of his own men were dead and Clint shot up. He figured that damn scout survived their attack and would be pissed as hell that we shot some more soldiers. He didn't think he wanted to be around when he showed up. He mentally counted up the men they had yesterday. They totaled twelve counting himself and Yancey. They were six now and two of them were wounded, Clint today and Mitch yesterday. At this rate he figured they would all be dead within twenty-four hours. He was brought back to the present by Yancey's voice.

"You look like you're in another world, Mason. Anything wrong?"

"What...huh no, nothing is wrong; just thinking about that damn scout."

"What about him?"

"Been thinking about that disaster a while ago with the Yankees. The more I think about it the more I think they were ready or damn near ready for us."

"And?"

"They were all in one spot, not scattered about the camp like they would have been if they were in their bedrolls." He paused a few seconds. "They were expecting us. Maybe we got there sooner than they thought we would, but they were out of their bedrolls. There was only a few seconds between the snapped limb and us attacking. Not enough time for them to get out of their bedrolls, get their boots on and grab their weapons. Yeah, they were expecting trouble...I know it."

"How in hell do you know they had their boots on?"

"They had to. They chased us for two hundred yards through the mesquite and cactus. Man couldn't run that far with thorns in his feet." Yancey mulled it over in his mind. He knew the man was right; he had already come to that conclusion.

"What's your point?"

"That damn Watkins again. He's smart Yancey, and he's hard to fool. I think we should just turn tail and hightail it out of the country as fast as we can...while we can."

Yancey grabbed him by the shoulder and jerked him around to where they were face to face. Mason was looking into the deadest eyes he had ever seen. No emotion showed...no feelings for anything. Yancey spoke in a threatening tone through gritted teeth.

"You will take orders from me," he raised his voice, "all of you will do what I say, when I say it. I'll shoot any man that tries to leave. IS

THAT CLEAR?" There was complete silence from the men. "I take that as a yes." No one spoke, some looked off and others hung their heads.

"To hell with you, Yancey," Mason said and turned to leave. Yancey jerked his knife out and drove it into the middle of the man's back. Mason stumbled forward, his right hand reaching over his shoulder trying to grab whatever was in his back. He stumble again, caught himself and turned, looking at Yancey. "You dirty sonofa..." he collapsed to his knees and then fell forward on his face. Yancey had his gun out, pointing it at the others. "Anyone else?" The men hung their heads, shuffling their feet. A couple looked at Mason. Each man knew they were with a madman and their time above ground was running out.

~~~

The sun wasn't half way across the sky when Tye and Dan came across the body of Mason.

"What in hell do you think caused this?" Dan asked, rolling the man over on his back.

"That's what happens when you cross Yancey." Dan looked up at Tye. "Don't take much to cross him either," he added. "Our men, his men, kids, women, it don't make a damn to him. There's Yancey's way or else." He nodded toward Mason, "That's the or else."

Dan shook his head, "Damn." Tye smiled and remounted Sandy just as Garrison and the others showed up.

Garrison looked down at Mason. "What happened?"

Dan, mounting his horse said, "He got the 'or else' from Yancey."

"Or else?" a surprised Garrison remarked. "What the hell does that mean?"

"If you don't agree with Yancey," Tye said, "You're asking to get gutted. Seen it before and so have you." Garrison looked as if he didn't know what Tye meant. "Remember when we had Yancey and his brother on the hill and when we got to the top, one of his men had been gutted like a deer?" Garrison looked off in the distance, rubbing his chin, remembering.

"Yeah, I tried to forget that sight; hadn't been able to though. The only thing worse was the sight of the pay wagon escort back in July when they were killed by the Vasquez gang and left for the buzzards."

"I've been out here all my life, Lieutenant, seen a lot of things, but the buzzards and the escort was the worse." Tye said reining Sandy around and heading out. "Let's go Lieutenant," he yelled, looking back over his shoulder. Dan caught up and pulled in beside him.

"You never told me the details about that pay wagon escort."

"Man would like to forget something like that, Dan." He thought for a moment before answering. "The men had been captured, lined up, executed and left where they lay. Didn't take long for the buzzards to move in ripping the bodies apart, eyes pecked out, guts scattered all over the place. A blind man would have gotten sick just because of the smell."

Dan said nothing. He shut his eyes, conjuring up the image of what that must have looked like. He felt a little sick. He understood now why Tye had been so unmerciful with members of the gang when they were caught. He thought Tye had gone a little far when he was questioning one of the gang in the guardhouse and pinned the man's hand to a table with his Bowie because he was slow answering a question. 'Think maybe he was justified,' he thought to himself.

"Tracks are pretty damn fresh, Dan, so keep your eyes open." Both men kicked their feet out of the stirrups. There was nothing worse than trying to get off a horse that has been shot, rearing up or falling and having your foot or feet hung up in them.

The lay of the land was conducive to having one's head shot off. Thick stands of cedar, sage, and juniper made one's remaining unseen, pretty easy. Throw in the mountains and the huge rocks, arroyos and a hundred other things one could name and it was a dangerous situation. It wasn't anything new to these men. They accepted the danger, actually enjoyed it. Not in a way that one would laugh, but in a way that made them feel alive, nerves on edge and enjoying every breath of air as if it was their last on earth. Doing the thing that most men wouldn't or couldn't do, was their way of life, what they were here for.

The trail led into a shallow stream and did not come out on the other side. "They are walking in the stream to cover their tracks, trying to slow us down some," Tye commented.

"Up stream or down?" Dan asked.

"Down stream is the fort, upstream some homesteaders. I think they need food, fresh horses, and ammunition and they plan to get it from the people living upstream, deeper into the hills," Tye said.

"My thoughts too," Dan said.

~~~

Yancey and Matt, lying behind some sage, watched the man and his two sons do their daily chores. The older man and one boy, probably his son, were clearing mesquite and sage from an area about fifty yards in front of the homestead and the youngest was shoveling manure from the corral. The house looked solid as the man obviously planned to be here for awhile. The shed and corral was built with the same care. They also noticed they each had a sidearm on their hip and a rifle always close by as they worked. The two men watching knew this was no pilgrim.

Yancey whispered, "There is an old saying about a man like this one. He's gonna be hard to take because he has been up the river and around the bend and would be tougher than nails."

"Heard that before," Matt whispered back. "About a year ago, Mason, Lewis, and me scouted out a family headed west in a wagon. Had two cows, a bull, and several head of goats and a cage full of chickens. Had two teenage sons, a daughter old enough and his wife. They were well heeled and you could tell they were confident and felt secure. Anyway, Mason rode back to camp and told Javier, who was the leader of our group of twenty or so men, about them and warned Javier they looked like they could handle themselves. Well, old Javier was not going to let anyone pass through the country."

"He and Mason and ten more men rode back to where me and Lewis lay, watching. He didn't even slow down, just took the men over the hill and charged the wagon, yelling like a bunch of Comanche. That old man and his son that was with him lay on the ground and both fired their rifles. Javier and the man next to him never knew what hit them. They both cart wheeled backwards, off their charging mounts. The youngest fired his Sharps, and damn if another didn't get knocked off his horse. The rest of the men kept charging. Puffs of dust where the bullets were hitting were all around the old man and his son as they lay on the ground. Both had their pistols out and knocked two more off their mounts. The men turned their mounts around and headed back up the hill. Then, the strangest damn thing I ever saw happened. The old woman stepped out of the wagon with a rifle, propped herself against the side of the wagon and fired. The rider, a man named Lester, tumbled off his horse. That shot had to be over a hundred yards and she hit him on a running horse. They killed six men in maybe thirty seconds. Guess they made it to wherever they were going because we sure as hell didn't bother them no more. Mason had said that that old man had been up the river and around the bend before that damn ignorant Javier got his self and five men killed."

"We need food and ammunition. We'll hit them at sunset, from behind the brush and rocks," Yancey said. "We won't go running in like a bunch of wild Comanche and with our repeaters, we should be able to take them."

Matt started to speak his objections but two things stopped him: one his belly told him he needed something in it and two, he remembered what happened to Mason. Both scooted backwards, careful not to raise any dust, until they could no longer see the old man and the boys.

~~~

Studying the tracks, Tye now knew where Yancey was headed and it sent a chill up his spine. They were headed for the McIntosh homestead. He told Dan where they were headed and drew a map on the ground. He told him to go back and get Garrison and don't stop till you get there.

"Where are you going?"

"Hell bent for leather to the McIntosh's place. I have to get there before they are all killed." Dan nodded his understanding and turning his mount around, headed back toward the patrol. Tye kicked Sandy in the flanks and headed in the opposite direction. He figured he was about five miles from the homestead. He was also thinking Yancey and his bunch were intent on getting food and supplies and figured the patrol was still far enough behind to be any cause for worry.

Tye had Sandy running in a draw he was familiar with and he lay low in the saddle. He gave Sandy free rein, letting him pick his way. He knew this draw he was in would cut his time to the homestead in half. He looked up at the setting sun and knew he was cutting it close.

It would be dark in less than an hour. If I was in Yancey's place, I would be getting ready and hit them with the setting sun behind me making it difficult for the man and his boys to be accurate. He thought of the last time he had sat down with the McIntosh family to eat. He smiled remembering the boys always asking him about his job. With the family way back in the hills and hardly ever seeing anyone, he was happy to bring them up to date on the news and catching Mrs. McIntosh up on the latest gossip that Rebecca keeps him up to date on. All the good times he had there came flooding back to him. They were good people and he just could not let anything happen to them.

He reined Sandy down to a trot and then a walk. He looked for signs that would tell him where he was in regards to the homestead. He was looking in every direction for a familiar landmark. About the time he thought maybe he had gone past the homestead he spotted the rock outcropping. If a man wanted to be able to find his way out here, or in the mountains, he had better remember landmarks to look for. The rock outcropping on a far away hill was such a place. It was black and stood out against the white rocks and sand of the hills. He knew this spot was a couple hundred yards from the homestead. He stopped Sandy and dismounted.

He tied Sandy to a cedar that had a good amount of grass around it, and then began to make his way up the side of the draw. Reaching the top, he lay on his belly, trying to get his bearings. It only took a minute of looking and he knew exactly where he was, two hundred yards in front of the homestead. Staying in a crouch, he moved toward the McIntosh homestead. No one was in the yard or the corral. Most people ate right before dark so he figured they were no exception. He stopped and let his eyes survey the area in front of the homestead.

There was sixty or seventy yards of cleared land all around the house which gave no cover to anyone trying to sneak in. Tye wasn't missing a bush or tree. He could not see anything but something was wrong. He kept still, moving only his eyes and a slight turn of the head. Sudden movement out here is noticeable real quick, so it was best to move slow and deliberate.

"No sound," Tye mumbled under his breath. A deathly silence surrounded him which was not natural. "No sound of birds or anything else." Even in this arid region, there was always a sound. He dropped to one knee, watching the area west of the house, studying every bush and rock. While he watched, a couple of turkeys ran from the cover, across part of the open ground and toward the south side of the house, toward Tye.

Tye knew something spooked them and he figured it was Yancey. He started moving very carefully and slowly to his left, intending to flank Yancey and his men…if they were there. He took every advantage of what cover there was and about ten minutes later, he was looking down at one of Yancey's men lying on the ground behind a cedar. Quickly scanning the area to the right and left of the man, he spotted two more. He figured Yancey must be farther to the left. To shoot at him, the old man would have to look directly into the sun. 'One thing about Yancey… he thinks only of Yancey,' Tye thought to himself. Tye made himself comfortable, waiting to see how things played out. He checked his rifle to make sure the barrel wasn't clogged from him scooting and crawling along the ground. He intended to fire the first shot to warn the McIntosh family but right now, he was content to wait. He looked up and nodded; thankful he wasn't too late to help his friends.

Chapter Eight

Rebecca laid her head back against the soft towel that served as a cushion against the edge of the steel tub. The hot water felt good and she was actually relaxed for the first time since Tye had left. Buff was sitting on the porch, his back against the door and four soldiers were scattered around the perimeter of the house making sure no one could harm her.

She thought of Tye and the last time they had made love. She shut her eyes and smiled. If only she could tell everyone how gentle and loving he was with her. She laughed because with his reputation of being so tough, no one would believe her. She thought of her parents and how she wished they were still alive and could have known him. She knew they would love him too.

Mrs. O'Malley had been over most of the day, keeping her company, trying hard to keep Rebecca's spirits up. She had a lot of experience coping with being alone since her husband was a career soldier. He had been away three years... three long years, during the war. She knew all about being lonesome and worrying whether Sergeant O'Malley was alive or not. Rebecca leaned on her a lot and Mrs. O'Malley always knew just what to say to help.

She decided she had been in the tub long enough since the water was getting cold. Standing up, she picked up the towel and rubbed herself dry. Putting her clothes on, she walked to the door and opened it.

"Feel bettur," Buff asked.

"Yes, I do, Buff. Thanks for the privacy."

"Wunt I shud emptee tha tub?"

"In awhile. Let's sit here and enjoy the sunset." She sat down beside Buff, putting her arm on his shoulder.

"Gonna be a purty wun with all them thar klouds laying thar in tha west when tha sun gits down behind them."

'Buff, do you think..."

65

"Now Rebecca, we dun had this heer conversation befo…several times ifn I member korrectly. Tye's fine." Rebecca laughed.

"I know. I won't ask again."

Buff looked at her and smiled. "Gud ta heer ya laugh again."

They watched as the sun disappeared behind the clouds resulting in a multitude of shades of color ranging from red, orange, black, yellow and several others.

"Purty, real purty," Buff said. Rebecca laid her head on his shoulder and prepared herself for another lonely night.

~~~

Tye saw the man closest to him turn his head to the left and shift he body. Then Tye, to his horror heard it too. The patrol was coming into view, heading straight to the homestead…and into a death trap. "What the hell is Dan thinking," Tye mumbled to himself. The door opened up and Mr. McIntosh stepped out on the porch and waved. Tye knew he had to warn the patrol. Against his morals about back shooting a man, he felt he had no choice. He sighted in on the man lying about forty yards below him and squeezed the trigger. The rifle bucked against his shoulder and the man jerked and rolled a few feet down the slope. Then, all hell broke loose. The repeating Henrys the outlaws used, opened up a murderous fire reigning down on Garrison and the patrol. Men were knocked off their mounts, others jumping to the ground and scrambling for cover.

Tye moved his barrel to the left and the Henry bucked again and another outlaw was rolling over and over down the slope. His eyes swept the area and he saw no other targets and his gaze went to the homestead. He saw smoke from rifles being fired from the door and windows. Looking toward the patrol he saw three men down. "Dammit," he expressed as he saw Dan being one of the men down.

It was suddenly quite, so quite that Tye could hear the men talking in the yard. He stood up and walked back to where Sandy was. Scooting down the bank on his butt, he landed almost at Sandy's hooves. The rocks and dust spooked Sandy and he was prancing around, straining against the reins. Tye's voice calmed him and he mounted up, heading back down the draw and then out, toward the homestead. He came in where he figured Yancey had been. Looking around he found another man that had been shot by the troopers or by the McIntosh men. He found another place where several spent cartridges lay. He figured this was where Yancey had lay but there was no sign of him. He trotted Sandy into the clearing after shouting who he was so he would not get himself shot.

Mrs. McIntosh was already outside, working on the men who had been shot. Tye quickly dismounted and ran to where Dan lay. He saw the bloody hole in his leg and another in his shoulder. Thankful he was alive; Tye kneeled down beside his long time friend and placed his hand on Dan's forehead. Dan's eyes opened and through gritted teeth that showed the pain spoke. "Can't believe I led those men in here; heard no shooting and figured maybe Yancey went somewhere else. Sorry, Tye." Tye patted him on the shoulder.

"Don't worry about it, Dan. We've all made mistakes. Just glad you're alive, old friend."

"What about the others?" Dan asked.

"Fixing to find out. Be right back." Tye walked over to where Garrison stood, blood running down his arm.

"Bad?" Tye asked.

"Just a flesh wound," he said, blood running through the fingers of his right hand that he held on the wound on his left shoulder. "We're hit hard, Tye," he said nodding toward the men on the ground. "Yeah, I know. I'll check and get back with you in a minute." Tye walked over to Mrs. McIntosh. She was working on Private Hunt who had a stomach wound. She looked up at Tye and shook her head, tears in her eyes. He walked over to Sergeant Norwood. He was unconscious with a crease in his skull just above the left ear.

"I think he will be okay," Mrs. McIntosh said nodding toward Norwood. "So will the scout. Both will be down awhile though." Tye nodded. He walked back over to Garrison.

"Hunt's dying, Lieutenant. Norwood and Dan are both out of things, same as you."

"How bad is Sergeant Norwood? He saved me, Tye. He jumped his horse in front of me and took the bullet."

"Has a crease in his skull. He'll be okay but gonna have a hell of a headache for awhile. I'm going to scout around up there," Tye said nodding his head toward the slope the outlaws were on. He walked off just as Mrs. McIntosh, wiping the tears from her eyes, walked over to take care of Garrison's arm.

"God sent you boys to save us," she said, tears welling up again in her eyes. Her husband walked up with the boys and they all hugged, then kneeled down and the old man prayed. Garrison took off his hat with his good arm. These are amazing people he thought as Mr. McIntosh prayed:

"Lord, we want to take time to thank you for these here soldier boys showing up just as the sons of Satan was going to smite us down.. I know them men's hearts are as black as sin, Lord, but there's good in every man. Please take a hard look at them before you pass judgment. We thank you again Lord for all the blessings you have bestowed on me and my family. Amen."

They stood up and hugged again and then each man shook Garrison's hand as the lady of the house doctored his arm.

"Better thank Tye," Garrison said. "His shot gave us a second or so of warning. He killed two of them. He's up there looking for sign of how many are left."

"Seems that man is almost always around when folks like us need him," Mr. McIntosh said. "He's the hand of God sent down to smite down the Philistine," he said arms outstretched to heaven.

"Come on now, Pa." Mrs. McIntosh said. "We all know Tye and he's just a man...a very good man."

"Here he comes now," William, Jr. said. Tye was coming down the slope, a scowl on his face. Arriving to the small group, he shook each man's hand and hugged Mrs. McIntosh.

"Thank the Lord we got here in time," Tye said holding her at arms length when he said it then pulled her close again. "That was a little bit too close."

"What did you find on the hill?" Garrison asked.

"Found four dead. Yancey wasn't one of them."

Garrison looked around. "Not much of a patrol left, Tye. What's the plan now?"

"You need to get the dead and wounded back to Clark. I'm going after Yancey."

"BY YOURSELF?" an astonished Garrison yelled.

"By myself," Tye calmly replied. "I will tell you something else, Lieutenant. I'm going to kill him too. I'm not bringing him in for trial and take another chance on him escaping. If I would have just killed him before, there would be several soldiers still alive and you, Dan, and Norwood would maybe be drunk over at Jim's saloon now instead of hurting like hell. Now get on the trail and when you get back tell Thurston that I requested he double the guard on Rebecca." He turned to Mrs. McIntosh. "Don't suppose you have any jerky and coffee you could spare?"

"We can find something for you, Tye. Come on in the house."

"Lieutenant, you can make the fort by morning if you get going." He stuck out his hand and Garrison took it in a firm handshake.

"You be careful, Tye."

"Always am, Lieutenant," he said smiling. "Now get going. You will be out of the hills in an hour or so and should have no trouble from then on." The McIntosh boys had rigged a travois for both Norwood and Dan. In a couple of minutes, what was left of the patrol had disappeared in the darkness. Tye walked into the homestead and immediately felt at home. The house was neat and clean and the smell of coffee was strong. There was something else too, a feeling one gets when he enters a home that is full of love. This was a good family...a good God fearing family. William Sr. brought him some jerky, biscuits, a little bacon, and some coffee.

"You're welcome to stay here tonight where it's comfortable," he said to Tye.

"I appreciate the offer but I'd better move on. Yancey will be moving and I'm getting farther behind."

"How can you track him tonight?"

"Can't. But I have a fair idea where he's going. I'm just going to head that way and when the sun comes up, see if I can find some tracks."

"Good luck to you and we're always in your debt." Tye shook the man's hand and tipped his hat to Mrs. McIntosh.

"Be by this way again," he said.

"You'll always be welcome." Tye nodded, tipped his hat again, mounted Sandy, and disappeared into the night.

~~~

69

It was about midnight when Garrison spotted the fire. He helped Dan sit up to see what he thought.

"Too big for Apache... probably the patrol that Phipps was sent to get."

"Stay here while I take a look." Garrison left on foot, then stopped and took off his spurs. It took him about ten minutes to get close enough to the fire to see who it was. Looking through the brush, he saw the uniforms of the cavalry. He hurried back to where Dan and Norwood were. Dan was waiting.

"It's the patrol. Let's get over there." He got Dan back on the travois and moved out.

"HELLO THE CAMP!" Garrison shouted. There was a mad scramble of men within the camp.

"IDENTIFY YOURSELF," a voice came from one of the sentries.

"Lieutenant Garrison from Clark."

"Come on in, Lieutenant," Lieutenant Paddock said. Garrison entered the light of the campfire.

"I have dead and wounded."

"Sergeant Baker."

"Yes Sir."

"Take care of the wounded."

"Yes Sir." Paddock turned back to Garrison.

"Step down Lieutenant. We've been looking for you." Garrison dismounted and Paddock saw his bloody shoulder. "You're wounded?"

"It can wait," He looked around the camp. Everything was exactly like the manual said it should be. He probably even had latrines dug. Paddock had been at the fort only a couple weeks and Garrison barely knew him. Thurston must have been desperate for officers to send him.

"Damn good to see you, Lieutenant." Garrison turned at the sound of his name.

"Phipps. Damn, I figured you would be getting drunk at Jim's by now." They shook hands.

"Couldn't leave my friends out here all alone," he said smiling. Looking around, he asked. "Where are they?"

Garrison looked at the ground. 'I'm the only one left standing...besides Tye." Phipps had a look of disbelief on his face.

"What...how... all dead?"

"Hunt is dead, rest wounded."

"Tye?"

"He's okay. He's after Yancey."

"YANCEY? He's after that sonofabitch all by himself?"

"That's the way he wanted it. We sure couldn't be much help with all the lead in us." Phipps pushed his hat farther back on his head, the brim almost pointing to the sky. "Lieutenant, you know Yancey like I do. He's the most vicious, demented man ever to set foot out here and he's plum crazy with hate for Tye."

"I know that Corporal. I know it as well as you do. I was on the patrol that brought him in...remember?" Phipps nodded.

"Yes Sir. I know that. Is anyone with Yancey?"

"If there is, it's no more than one. Rest were killed at the McIntosh place."

"McIntosh? That's Tye's friend in the hills."

"We got there maybe a minute or so before Yancey's bunch was going to hit them."

"Are they okay?

"They are all fine." Phipps nodded then turned to Paddock.

"We need to start early, Sir. Tye's gonna need us sure as hell."

"We'll start early, Corporal." Paddock stated. Phipps turned and walked away.

"He's kinda worried about, Mr. Watkins?' Paddock questioned.

"He's one of Tye's best friends. He's also a hell of a soldier, Lieutenant. You being new out here, I'd listen to him if I was you."

"The major told me to listen to Tye and you're telling me to listen to a corporal." He spit on the ground. "Don't do a man any good to have rank around here." He started to walk away but was spun around by a strong grip on his shoulder. Garrison got up into his face.

"I'm gonna give you some good damn advice, Lieutenant, and you better listen or you won't live to see your next birthday. Tye has saved these troopers asses no telling how many times and they love him. You show any disrespect to him and I'll guarantee you a short life because one of them will blow your damn pious head off the first time you are in a battle and say it was the Apache. These men out here are not like your buddies at the Academy or the soldiers with the soft asses back east. These men are hard. They have been out here for awhile and they have seen and done things that you could not imagine. Some fought in

71

the War, some for the Confederates and some for the Yankees. Some are ex-buffalo hunters and trappers. They don't like fresh snotty nosed Lieutenants who think they know every thing. They have seen too many of their friends killed by officers that don't know squat. I know what I am talking about Lieutenant because I was just like you a few months ago. I was at the top of my class and figured I knew everything there was to know. Come to find out, all that book learning hasn't helped me one damn bit out here. The Apache and the bandits never read the 'Rules of War'…they make their own and are damn good at it. Men like Tye were born out here. He has been fighting Apache and bandits all his life. Hell, he killed his first Apache in a knife fight when he was fifteen"

Garrison backed off, his anger cooled. "Lieutenant, the major is trying to steer you straight when he told you to listen to Tye. He thinks like an Apache, can track better than most of them, can handle any fight whether with fist, knife, or gun. He can be meaner than a she wolf with pups but, when you are his friend, he'll give his life for you. You will do well to listen to him and the men that's been out here for awhile…that is if you want to live. I'll shut up now, I've spoke my mind." He pointed his finger at Paddock and in a threatening tone said "You do what you want but don't let your arrogance get any of my friends killed." He turned, walked to his bedroll and lay down, pulling the wool blanket up to his chin. He laid there his anger gone and thinking he probably said too much.

Paddock walked to his bedroll and lay down, but sleep didn't come. He was thinking over what Garrison had said and realized it was almost the same speech the major had given him. He lay there thinking. He sure as hell didn't want to get 'accidentally' shot by his own men. Maybe he had been a little arrogant. He would change that.

~~~

It was a cold camp. Yancey and Tom lay in their bedrolls, bellies growling. Tom was reflecting on what had happened. "How did those soldiers catch up to us so quick?"

"Blind luck on their part. They didn't know we were there. I think they knew where that homestead was and was just making sure they were safe."

"Some of those shots, the ones that killed Matt and Lewis came from behind us."

Yancey raised up. "You sure about that?"

"Hell yes. The first shot came from there and took out Matt. It also warned the patrol."

"WATKINS," Yancey yelled. "That sonofabitch Watkins. It had to be him. Damn him. Seems like he's been a thorn in my butt my whole life."

"Maybe he has. The only thing I care about is getting some stinking food in my belly. The last time I was this hungry was in that damn Yankee prison camp."

"We'll find some in the morning. There's more homesteads and that bastard Watkins can't watch all of them. Try and get some shuteye. The horses will let us know if anyone gets close."

Gary McMillan

Chapter Nine

With no moon, it was a little dangerous traversing the hills and arroyos causing Tye to call it a day and make a cold camp. He shivered some as the nights were no longer just cool, they were becoming cold. He unsaddled Sandy, gave him his usual rubdown, fed him oats and poured a little water in his hat for him. With Sandy taken care of, he found the smoothest place he could find on the rocky ground and spread his bedroll and stretched out. The wool blanket removed the chill from his body and he gradually relaxed, looking up at the stars. With no moonlight to hinder their luster, they were beautiful, looking like a thousand sparkling diamonds on a black velvet background.

Tye lay there looking at the wondrous sky, mulling over the days events and his plans for tomorrow. He figured at daylight he would ride to his right for a mile or so to see if he could pick up Yancey's tracks. If none were found, he would backtrack to this spot and go left for a mile or so. He would have to find tracks one way or the other.

As tired as he was, he couldn't go to sleep. He tried to think what Yancey would do. He knew they had to have some food. I don't think he would risk a shot to kill a deer which would give his location away. He will probably try to sweet talk his way into a homestead, maybe asking for something to eat. Once inside he'd kill the folks and take what he needed.

A sudden thought came to him, one that sent chills up his spine. What if Yancey turned south and headed to the fort. Fear grabbed hold and his heart throbbed heavily in his chest. His breath came in short gasps for a moment. Then he relaxed, realizing he would not do that, not yet anyway. He figured Yancey knew that everyone at the fort would still be alert for him or any other civilians that made an attempt to come onto the fort. If Yancey was smart, he would stay in the hills till things calmed down some.

He thought of what that bastard would do to Rebecca if he did catch her. A lump formed in his throat at that thought. He didn't think that would happen with Buff and the soldiers there. But something his pa had always preached to him entered his mind. "Always prepare for the worse, Tye, and if it don't happen, be thankful." He had taken that approach many times in the past. Sometime later, he drifted off to sleep.

First light found Tye traveling north, looking for any sign of Yancey's passing. The ground was rocky and it was going to take all his skills to find sign. His best hope was that Yancey had been moving fast. A horse trotting or running would leave sign that a walking horse would not. After an hour of climbing in and out of arroyos, getting down on his hands and knees looking for any sign, he decided to stop and backtrack to where he started. The sun was midway to its zenith when he found where he camped last night

He dismounted, loosened the girth on the saddle and sat down to eat a piece of jerky. He was on the side of a hill and had an open view across a canyon to the west. Chewing his jerky he was just fixing to take a drink from his canteen when he saw it...or thought he saw it. Something flashed on the hill maybe two miles away. Not to many things out here that wasn't man made reflected sunlight. But did he see it or was it his imagination. It had flashed for only an instant. He sat the canteen down and stared in the area he thought he saw the flash. For a full minute he watched and saw nothing else. Standing up, he cinched the saddle and mounted Sandy. Deciding to forgo the idea of going south, he decided to take the chance he had seen something and headed there.

~~~

Yancey and Tom were moving a lot slower today, taking the time to cover their tracks. They didn't have time to do that last night. They only wanted to put distance between them and whatever was left of the patrol. The anger Yancey had last night had been replaced by determination, as if he needed more, to kill Watkins. He was thirty-five years old. He had been in more fights than he could remember, killed more people than he could remember, but he had never actually hated anyone...till now. He wanted to kill that damn scout more than anything in the world but he was experienced enough to know that a man full of hate can sometimes get careless. He wasn't going to let that happen to him.

Topping a hill they could see a homestead in the valley below with smoke coming from the chimney.

"Well lookee there, Yance. Food is on the table." They both studied the homestead and the lay of the land around it. Like most out here, the homesteaders had cleared the area around their homes for over a hundred yards, providing no cover for attacking Indians or bandits.

"How are we going to handle this?" Tom asked.

"Thinking about that," Yancey answered. "We don't need a fire fight. That would attract some unwanted attention. I think one of us might be able to get in there but two might not be welcome. I'll go down there and try to get their confidence and get inside. When its clear, I'll signal you."

"Be careful but do it quick. My old belly is hurting something fierce." Yancey rode down the slope toward the house.

"HELLO THE HOUSE," he shouted. The door opened and a man stepped out holding a rifle in front of him.

"WHO ARE YOU?" he hollered back. Yancey rode a little closer, his arms out, away from his gun.

"Bill...Bill Johnson," he said.

"Don't know you," the man answered.

"Just passing through. Thought maybe I could get a bite to eat."

"You alone?" Yancey dismounted and took off his hat, holding it in front of him.

"Just a cowpoke, sir...a hungry one. Be willing to work for it." He said a big smile on his face.

"No need. We got some extra so come on in." The old man lowered his rifle and walked into the home with Yancey on his heels. Yancey noticed the house was neat and clean, even with a dirt floor. A small, gray haired lady stuck out her hand.

"My name is Katie and this is our son, Jesse." Jesse looked about thirteen or fourteen years old. The old man looked to be about fifty. The old man stuck out his hand.

"My name is ..."he never finished as Yancey shot him in the chest. At this range, the force of the bullet knocked him off his feet and against the wall where he hung there for a couple of seconds before sliding to the floor. Yancey turned and the boy was grabbing a rifle off the wall. Yancey shot him in the back and he stumbled once, and then fell face down on the dirt floor. The old woman screamed and he slapped her hard across the mouth, knocking her down. He picked up a knife off the table and stabbed her in the back as she was getting up. She collapsed back on the floor, tried to get back up and fell again. She didn't move anymore.

Yancey walked outside took off his hat, and waved it at Tom, signaling him to come on in. He turned to go back in then jerked his head around and looked up the slope. Where was Tom? He scanned the area around the home, no one was there. "What the hell?" He went back into the house and started gathering the things he needed: food, ammo, an extra rifle, another canteen, blankets, and a few cooking utensils. He walked out to the corral and roped one of the horses to carry all the supplies on. Leading the horse back he loaded all the supplies in two bags and tied them on the horse. Mounting his horse, he rode off leading the pack horse with a halter rope.

Tom watched from a far away hill. He waited for thirty minutes to be sure Yancey wasn't coming back then rode down to the homestead. Entering, he paid no mind to the bodies of the people. He was grabbing food. He sat down at the table and ate his fill of biscuits and bacon. He even found a jug of whiskey. After eating his fill, he grabbed what food he could find that Yancey hadn't taken and started out the door. He stopped in his tracks, his mouth still full of biscuit and stared at the man sitting on a large sorrel.

Tye sat on Sandy, his rifle laying across the saddle, pointing right at Tom. Tom spit out the biscuit. "Who the hell are you?"

"The man that's going to kill you; if you make a wrong move." Tom knew he was a dead man if he tried anything.

"Where's Yancey?" Tye asked.

"Dunno," Tom said. "I knew what he was going to do to these people and I didn't like it. Didn't approve of him trying the other cabin either but he's a man you don't disagree with. Mason did and Yancey stabbed him the back. When he came down here I left, didn't want no more to do with him. He's a crazy sonofabitch. After he left, I waited awhile and then came down to get something to eat. I was half starved. When we met up with him we figured we were gonna get shot or hung if we stayed with him. He's just a hard one to shuck if you want to stay alive a little longer. I'm the only one left alive."

"Where did he go?"

"Headed northwest, over that hill yonder," Tom said nodding.

"Did he say where he was going?"

"No, but he ain't going far. He's bound and determined to kill some scout at Clark by the name of Watkins. We all told him he was crazy but there's no reasoning with him. Said he was gonna get that man's purty wife and pleasure himself in front of him before he killed them both. He's plum crazy mister." Tom started toward his horse. "What's your name?"

"Watkins…Tye Watkins." Tom stopped in his tracks. He dropped the supplies and turned toward Tye knowing he was probably a dead man.

"You going to kill me?"

"Depends on whether you help me or not."

"How can I help you? I told you what direction he headed." He turned slightly away from Tye and in one quick motion turned back, pulling his gun from his holster. Tye was expecting it and simply pulled the trigger of the rifle that was already pointing at Tom. The bullet hit him high in the chest spinning him around. Tye levered another shell in the Henry and fired again as Tom, after spinning around, was raising his gun to fire. The second bullet hit him square in the chest knocking him backwards. He was dead before he hit the ground.

Tye dismounted and walked over to him. Using his toe he flipped Tom over on his back to make sure he was dead. He walked to the house, paused to take a deep breath, exhaling slowly. He steeled himself for what he knew he would find inside. No one, no matter how many times they saw it, could see people murdered in cold blood and not feel sick. Tye looked around and then checked just to make sure they were dead. Walking out to the shed, he found a shovel and looked for a place to dig graves. He should be after Yancey, but he could not leave these people for the varmints. They deserved a decent burial. As hard as he could try, he could only dig three holes about a foot and a half deep in the rocky ground. He wrapped the bodies in blankets and placed them in the holes. He rounded up rocks to place on top to keep the coyotes and other animals from digging them up. He didn't know what to say but looked up at the sky.

"Lord, I didn't know these folks but I know you did. I believe they were good people and believed in you. Take them to your bosom Lord." He kneeled down and placed his hand on the boy's grave. "Didn't get much of a chance in life did you, son? I will avenge you and your mother and father, this I swear." He stood up. "Rest in peace."

He stood as he swallowed the lump in his throat, and walked over where the sacks lay that Tom had. He emptied them on the ground and picked up some coffee, biscuits and jerky. He placed them in his saddle bags and mounted Sandy. He looked at the ridge that Yancey went over. "Your time is running out Yancey," he mumbled out loud and headed out. It was mid afternoon and he had several hours of daylight left. He made the top of the ridge, dismounted, and studied the tracks so he would recognize them if they mingled with others. The horse Yancey rode had a cracked shoe. This could help if the horse became lame. Tye immediately dismissed that as being a good thing because it meant that the bastard would probably kill someone for another horse. He toed the stirrup and swung into the saddle. He kicked Sandy in the flanks and followed the tracks, knowing that he was in the fight of his life with this mad man and only one would walk away.

~~~

Yancey had ridden about four miles since leaving Tom and the homestead. He thought he had heard a couple shots from that direction but knew they were way off. He was traveling slower than he would like, but he was an experienced soldier and was taking time to cover his tracks. He rode only on the rocky ground when he could and had traveled about a half mile in a shallow creek before coming out, again on some rocks. He was sure Watkins was back there, following him like some damn bloodhound. He knew that he would meet him for a final fight before long. He wanted it to be in a place and time that he wanted, not an accidental meeting. He still could not figure what happened to Tom unless he just got cold feet and ran away. That was hard to believe since he had seen him in action. He knew he wasn't afraid. Hell, maybe the stress finally got to him. He had seen that happen before to a brave man. A man could be a fighting machine one minute and a shaking shell of himself the next. He reined his mount to a halt and dismounted. He walked off a ways to relieve his bladder. When through, he walked back to the packhorse and grabbed some jerky out of one of the sacks. He remounted and chewed the jerky while riding. He looked over his shoulder several times during the next hour or so but saw nothing. "He's there…he's back there somewhere, I can feel it, DAMMIT, I CAN FEEL IT," he shouted out loud. His horse nickered, twitched his ears, and looked back at him. "Damn! I'm talking to my horse now." He laughed…a nervous laugh.

Gary McMillan

Chapter Ten

L ieutenant Paddock and the patrol were having a hard time following Tye's tracks. Phipps was a hell of a soldier, tougher than nails, but he was finding out he was not a tracker. He had lost the trail over an hour ago. Paddock was upset by this but being totally lost himself, he kept quiet. He was doing his best to do what he told himself last night, listen and learn and don't make an ass out of himself.

Phipps came riding back and up to the Lieutenant. He took off his kerchief and then his hat. He wiped his face with the kerchief and then his hat band before looking up at Paddock. "I've lost it, Sir. Plum damn lost it." He looked up at the sun. "It's mid afternoon, Sir. Why don't you let me pick a man and we can cover twice the ground while you and the patrol take a break. The horses need it."

"Pick your man, then" Paddock said. "SERGEANT."

"Here, Sir."

"Have the men dismount. We'll take a short break."

"Yes Sir." The sergeant turned back to his men. "Thirty minute break." The men straightened up and waited. "DISMOUNT." They stepped from the saddle, some rubbing their butts. All loosened their saddle girths and gave their horses some water from their hats before they took care of themselves.

Phipps had his man, Private Jackson, with him. He told him to go south for a mile or so and report back any tracks. Phipps went north. Paddock sat on a rock wondering what the hell he was doing out here. Been here two weeks, did not know any of the enlisted men, did not have a clue on how to get back the fort and looking for a scout he had never met. Sergeant Baker sat down beside him.

"You okay, Lieutenant?"

Paddock nodded. Baker said, "You know Lieutenant, you're doing fine for your first patrol." Paddock looked at him, a dubious look on his face.

"I'm serious, Lieutenant. I have been on patrols with officers like you making their first venture into this here country. Some were arrogant, some were lost, others tried to learn from their men who had been here. I think you are the latter."

Paddock stared off into space, looking but seeing nothing. "I had a pretty good lecture from Thurston before I left and from Garrison last night." He laughed. "Told me I had better not get any of his friends killed with my arrogance…and stupidity."

Baker slapped his leg and laughed. "All the new officers get that speech. The officers that take it to heart make it…those that don't usually are gone pretty quick…or dead. Garrison is a good officer."

"Tell me about this scout, Watkins. I've been hearing stories about him since I arrived in San Antonio before coming to Clark."

"Hell, Lieutenant. That could take forever. I will say this first. Whatever you heard is probably true. He's the best scout in the whole damn army. I've been on the plains chasing the Comanche and the Sioux before the War and out here chasing Apache since. Seen a lot of scouts over the years; ain't a one of them even close to Tye. His pa was a pretty well know mountain man you know. Rubbed shoulders with Bridger and all of the ones you read about. He even had a few of those dime novels that are popular back east written about him. He started teaching Tye tracking, shooting, fighting, and every other skill to survive out here since Tye was old enough to walk. Tye killed his first Apache with a Bowie when he was fourteen or so. That man back at the fort, Shakespeare, was a mountain man and his best friend was Tye's pa. He came here to meet his friend's son. Hear tell he's seventy-one years old but you wouldn't want to cross him." He took a drink from his canteen.

"I'll tell you something else, Lieutenant. There's not a man on the fort that has not had their butt saved by that man… some of us more than once. There's not a man on the fort that would not do whatever it took to protect Tye's wife. He brought in this man we're chasing, Yancey, about a month ago; meanest, most vicious killer that's ever been born. Killed people just for the joy of watching them suffer and die. He swore he would escape and kill Tye and his wife. He made good the first part, the escape. We are hoping we can help Tye keep the second part from happening."

Paddock nodded his head. "Sounds like a good idea to me." He smiled and shook the Sergeants hand. "Thanks for the information." He looked west, where Phipps and Jackson had rode off to. 'They should be coming back soon,' he thought to himself.

~~~

Tracking Yancey was slow going. Tye would find a scratched rock, broken limb, or some bent grass, and every once in awhile a track, but they were few and far between. "Knows something about covering his tracks, doesn't he Sandy." He reined up and dismounted. He stood beside Sandy, staring in the distance and scratching Sandy between the ears. "It may take us a little longer but we'll get him." Sandy nickered and shook his head causing Tye to smile, "Damn if you don't understand every word I say." He looked north and saw something he didn't want to see. "Looks like some weather coming," he mumbled to himself, "Could be a little snow if the temperature drops enough." He checked to make sure his slicker, jacket, and bedroll was secure. He figured he had about an hour till sundown and he needed to find a place to hole up by then, He thought Yancey would be doing the same. All wild animals have enough sense to get out of storms and Yancey certainly fit the bill as an animal.

He topped a small hill and found a few tracks, plain as day. 'He's looking for a place and getting careless..,' he thought to himself. Tye figured he was a little over three hours behind him. He looked at the lay of the land and did what his pa had taught him. He mentally put himself in the place of the person he was tracking. He tried to figure out what he would do if he was in their shoes. Looking around, he spotted a cut about a mile away. The walls of the cut were steep, rocky and may have a cave or at least, a place where rocks were large enough to maybe block out the worse of the storm. He figured Yancey was already through the cut. His tracks were headed straight for it. Suddenly, a thought came to him and he reined Sandy in dismounting so quick, his feet hit the ground before Sandy came to a complete halt.

'That damn cut is also the perfect place to ambush a man,' he thought to himself. He tied Sandy to a large cedar but left enough rope that he could scrounge some of the short grass up to eat. He took the Henry out of the saddle scabbard. "Be back in a few minutes ole boy," he said patting Sandy on the neck. He headed toward the cut...real careful like. He moved from bush to bush and rock to rock, not running in a straight line. He knew Yancey was an old southern boy and was probably a crack shot. At the mouth of the cut, he studied both sides, especially the north side. If Yancey was smart, and he knew he was, he would be on that side so the storm would blow over him. He found his tracks going into the cut. He decided to work his way around and up the south side and maybe be able to spot where he was...if he was there. It's possible he had already gone through the cut before he noticed the storm moving in and didn't want to backtrack because he figured he was being followed.

Tye had reached the top of the cut and crawled on his belly to the edge and taking his hat off, hiding behind some clumps of cactus, studied the north cliff. The cut was no more than a hundred yards long and he was almost in the middle so he could see the whole north wall. There were some places to get out of the storm and he studied them and every other possible place a man could hide. He saw nothing. He stood up and scrambled back down to where Sandy was. He was going into the cut and find a hole. He glanced up at the darkening sky. "We don't have much time, Sandy." Sandy sensed the urgency in Tye's voice and was skittish, anxious to be on the move. "It's okay, boy. It's okay." His voice had a calming affect and Sandy stopped stomping around long enough for Tye to mount him.

It didn't take Tye long to find a good place to put up for the night. It wasn't a cave but about five feet up the north wall, a huge boulder had fallen sometime in the past and been swept away over time by floodwaters. A fair sized cavity was left in the wall. Sandy was able to scramble up, with Tye's help pulling on the reins, to the indention left by the boulder. It was bigger than Tye expected and the overhang might just keep them both dry. Tye scrambled back down to the floor of the cut and started throwing driftwood up to the cleft.

It was beginning to rain by the time he figured he had enough. He placed some rocks in a circle and built himself a small fire. The back wall would deflect some of the heat making the place tolerable. It was raining fairly hard now, but both Sandy and himself were staying dry. He unrolled his bedroll against the back wall and crawled under the wool blanket. He placed his slicker over the bottom half to make sure it stayed dry. He had taken his gun belt off and his pistol out of the holster. He held it in his hand under the blanket and had his Henry lying beside him, also under the blanket. He reached over and added a couple sticks to the fire, lay back and dozed off, depending on Sandy to wake him if anyone or anything came around. Sometime during the night he woke up and added wood to the fire and noticed it was snowing. That was good news and bad news. The bad news was his old tracks would be covered but the good news was when he moved now he would leave tracks. Tye just had to find where he holed up. He tried to back to sleep but it would not come.

He lay there watching the flakes coming down, thankful there was just enough of a north wind to keep most of them off Sandy and him. His thoughts drifted back to another night like this many years ago. Pa and him had been caught too far away from home to get back and had holed up in a place almost like this, but deeper with a lot more overhang. He lay there listening to pa tell of the winters in the Rockies. "A man would go maybe six or seven months and never see grass," he would say. "Seen it so cold one time that old Buff and me were talking and had to wait till it warmed up some so our words would thaw out and we could hear what the other said." Tye found that one a little hard to swallow now, but when you were a kid; you soaked in and believed everything your pa said. Pa was a good man, a well respected man, but he was a better father just as his mother was a great mother. A man could not have asked for better. He swallowed the lump in his throat and tried to think of something else.

~~~

Earlier, just before dusk, Yancey found a place to hole up. He found a spring that had some huge oaks around it and sometime in the past, one had been uprooted by a storm. It had left a huge hole in the ground and had fallen almost due north. Its roots, looking like giant arms reaching toward the sky were spread out in all directions, and maybe ten foot off the floor of the hole. It wasn't the perfect place but he would stay pretty much dry and the wind would be blocked. He picketed his horse at the far end of the hole and gathered some wood for the night. He wished he had gone back to the cut. He had seen two or three places there that were better than this but he was afraid he would run into Watkins and what was left of the patrol. He hadn't hung around to see how devastated the patrol had been in the shoot out and had no idea Tye was following him alone. He built himself a small fire and pulled the heavy coat's collar up around his ears. He was thankful he had seen the coat at the homesteader's place he had ransacked. He would be pretty damn miserable about now if he hadn't. He lay down beside the fire and fell into a light sleep thinking about that stinking blue-belly scout.

~~~

Lieutenant Paddock lay in his bedroll thinking of what he should do. Phipps and Jackson had not been able to pick up Tye's trail and now, with the snow, there would be none. He starred at the falling snow, thinking of home. Back home near Washington, snow this time of the year was commonplace, but here, it was not and all were miserable. They had not been able to find shelter other than the stand of oaks they were under. The trees kept most of the falling snow off them but did nothing to hinder the cold wind that crept under the blankets and collars of the soldiers. It was going to be a long and miserable night for all.

Phipps came over with two cups of steaming coffee and sat down.

"Sorry about the tracks, Lieutenant. The only thing I can figure out is that Tye didn't think to mark a trail because he didn't know we were right behind him."

Paddock nodded. "I figure the same."

"What are we going to do?"

"Been thinking on that, Phipps. I think at first light, we'll split into four groups of three men each. We'll spread out about a quarter mile apart and head west. Covering that much ground, we should stumble onto someone's tracks in the snow. That's the only plan I can come up with. We'll give it most of the day and if we haven't found anything, we'll head back to the fort."

"Are you sure you want to do that, Sir?"

"No, I don't. But unless you have a better plan, I don't know what else to do."

"Damn." Phipps said standing up. "Think some more, Sir. We've got to find Tye." He walked over to his bedroll and lay down pulling the wool blanket up to his chin. "Damn." He mumbled again. He knew the Lieutenant was right in heading back if they could find no tracks. This was a big country and a man could get mighty lost in it if he had a mind to. He figured Yancey had a mind to and Tye was following him. Maybe it's a moot point to be worrying about. The Lieutenant is probably right. Spread out like that, we should find the tracks.

~~~

Back at headquarters, Thurston was concerned about things. Garrison, with what was left of the patrol, had ridden in before dusk. The report he received from Garrison didn't help his disposition any. Of all the outlaws to get away, it had to be that murdering Yancey. "YANCEY." He spit out the name in disgust. Thurston was a man who never let feelings get in the way of his judgment. He tried to never hate the men he fought or hunted. He understood the Apache and had no dislike for them… unlike others in command at different forts who felt the only good Apaches was a dead Apache. Things were tough out here and in some way, he understood the bandits. Yancey was a different breed. He was pure evil and maybe, Thurston had thought, was the devil himself and come from hell to kill, rape, and pillage the good people out here. He laughed at the thought for an instant before he realized it was no laughing matter. This man had to be found.

He was leaving to go to his quarters when Shakespeare showed up. They shook hands.

"Hurd abut tha patrol, Major. Anee more news kum down frum tha hills?"

"No more news, Buff. All I know, there was a fight and all the bandits were killed except Yancey. Garrison and the patrol were shot up pretty good."

"Damn man has mor lives than a kat." Buff said. "Hurd ya had anuther patrol out thar ta try and help Tye."

"That's right. I hope they can but I did not have a scout available. Corporal Phipps said he knew the country and could find Tye and Garrison. He left with Lieutenant Paddock and ten men. Phipps found what was left of the patrol but Tye had already left to follow Yancey. Paddock left following Tye."

"This heer Lieutenant Paddock a gud man? "Don't' recall heering his name befo."

89

"That's what's bothering me, Buff. I don't know if he is or not. He's new out here and don't know squat. I thought Phipps would find Garrison and Tye and he could learn from them. No amount of book learning prepares a man for this country. You know that. I never dreamed that when he found the patrol, they would be shot to hell and no one left standing that could continue."

"Don't ya go blamin yourself nune, Major. Who wud had tho't tha. We kan hope tha found Tye an ar tagether now, while we ar talking and wurring abut it."

"I hope so, Buff." There's nothing we can do but pray about it and wait till we hear something. I figure they are getting some snow up in those hills and things are pretty miserable for them."

Buff shook his hand. "Thangs will be okay, Majur. Guess I had bettur git bac to tha house and luk aft'r Becca." Thurston watched him leave and a plan started forming in his mind and he wished he had thought of it before. He had a tracker here, probably as good as Tye and he didn't think to send him with Paddock "Damnation," he said out loud. If need be, he would send Buff with a couple of men. Buff could find Tye if anyone could.

Chapter Eleven

With the coming of dawn, Tye was looking at low hanging, gray clouds that looked so heavy with snow and ice that they could empty at anytime. It wasn't snowing now but it was cold, probably a few degrees below freezing. From the looks of the sky, it was not going to warm up much. His fire was down to glowing coals. He reached and put some more wood on and in a moment, the fire flared up. He lay under the wool blanket, dreading to get out long enough to put on his moccasins. He reached out and put his moccasins close to the fire. "Be nice to put these old feet in something warm instead of starting out cold." Sandy nickered and shook his head, throwing some ice that had formed in his mane. He shook his withers and shoulders telling Tye it was chilly and the saddle blanket would feel good. At least this was what Tye figured he was saying. Tye smiled, raised up and threw the wool blanket off. He put on his moccasin boots that were warm and felt good to his cold toes. He stood up and shivered before he put his coat on then threw the blanket on Sandy. Sandy nickered, looked back at Tye and nodded his head as if to say, "It's about time." Tye laughed this time. He loved this horse.

Only a couple inches of snow had fallen, but there was a dangerous layer of ice below it. He took his coffee pot and filled it to the top with snow and set it on the rocks by the fire. He added a handful or two of snow as it melted. When it was boiling he dropped in some coffee grounds and let it boil for a minute. Setting the pot away from the fire he dropped in some cold water from his canteen that had been by the fire. The little bit of cold water settled the grounds to the bottom of the pot. He poured himself a cup and leaned back against the warm cliff to think things out.

He figured Yancey was doing the same thing, dreading to get out in the cold. From the last sign he had found, he figured he was two to three hours behind him. He could mount Sandy now and probably make up some ground but he also could stumble into where he was holed up and get himself shot. "What the hell," he said to Sandy. "Let's go." He saddled up Sandy, rolled up his bedroll and put his camp utensils away. He led Sandy down the five or so feet to the floor of the draw. It was damn slick and Sandy stood still, probably thinking whether he wanted to try this or not. Tye wasn't going to mount him and take a chance of him or Sandy being injured in a fall. He led him out of the cut and was glad that the breeze was in his face. He could smell the smoke from a camp before he stumbled into it. He carried the Henry in his gloved left hand and had Sandy's reins in his right.

He searched the terrain with his eyes, looking for anything that could be a hint of trouble. There was not a sound other than his feet and Sandy's hooves crunching the frozen snow. Even the birds had disappeared. The slight breeze blowing in his face had his cheeks red and had him shivering under the jacket. He was cold, tired, and a little hungry since he was saving his jerky in case this ended up being a long chase. These feelings were nothing to him though. Most of his life he had very little. Even as a youngster, it seemed now that he was always this way. There was plenty of love between his parents and him which made the hardships not so noticeable. Then again, he never needed much. He never owned more than two pair of pants and maybe three shirts at any one time in his life…that is till he married Rebecca. He now had more clothes than he needed. He told Rebecca to slow down but since Mrs. O'Malley had showed her how to sew, she spent a lot of time making herself and Tye clothes.

Suddenly Sandy's ears flickered and he whinnied. Tye smelled it at the same time… smoke. He dropped to one knee behind a snow covered cedar just as a whisper of a bullet went by where his head had been a second before. The report of the rifle came an instant later. He knew the next shot would be at the cedar which offered very little protection. He dove to the left rolling behind a boulder as bullets sprayed snow and ice all around him. He looked back at Sandy knowing what that sonofabitch was fixing to do. He jumped up and grabbing the dangling reins, ran with Sandy about ten feet behind some large cedars that offered a little more protection for Sandy. He ran, jumped, and rolled back behind the boulder he was behind earlier. He could see better from here than he could back in the cedars. He had no idea where the shot came from other than somewhere in front of him. The only sound was his heavy breathing from the excitement and exertion of the last minute. His sense of hearing was tuned in for any sound. He knew if Yancey was close, any time he moved Tye would hear him on the snow. A minute went by, then five, and still no sound.

~~~

Yancey knew he had missed the instant he pulled the trigger. He had Watkins' head in his sights and just as he fired, the head disappeared. Not only was this damn man good and tough, he was lucky as hell. He knew something warned him but didn't know what. It was a standoff now and he was in no mood to lay here and freeze his butt in one. He slid quietly back down the slope to his camp. Got everything together and prepared to leave. He wrapped his horses' hooves in cloth to cut down the sound. They would not stay on long but maybe long enough for him to put a little distance between him and Watkins. He wondered where the others were as he walked the horses away.

~~~

Tye waited another five minutes, listening for any sound. Hearing none, he bunched his muscles and sprang from behind the boulder, sprinting and sliding about fifty feet closer to the hill. He saw another large boulder and running, slid in behind it. Breathing heavy, he lungs hurting from the cold air he sat perfectly still until his breathing returned to normal. He took a quick look over the boulder and then ducked back down. He moved to the left a couple feet and again took a quick look before ducking back down. He again sprinted ahead, this time to the base of the hill. No shots were fired in his direction. He stood up, his Henry braced against his shoulder, ready to fire. Nothing moved. He walked to the top and looked down on the abandoned camp. The protection from the storm had been fair at best he figured. "Bet you got a little chilly and wet last night, Yancey," he mumbled under his breath.

He walked down to the camp, looking around before going to the far side and saw where Yancey had left, but then the tracks disappeared. He stood there looking all around trying to figure out how they just disappeared. Kneeling down and taking a closer look, he smiled.

93

'Yancey, you sly fox,' he thought to himself. He could tell the horses hooves had been wrapped to cut down the sound. He followed the marks until he came to the first wrap and a couple steps later the second. The tracks were plain now, and the horses' were moving fast... too fast on this surface. Yancey was asking for trouble. He could see where both horses were slipping. The second horse was not carrying much weight. Tye figured this to be a pack horse. He had not known this before because of the lack of tracks that he had found on the rocks where Yancey had stayed most of the time before the storm moved in. He hurried back to Sandy and mounting up, followed the tracks.

~~~

The patrol had not found any tracks. Paddock and Phipps were at a loss as to how two men and horses could travel through this country and not leave any sign of their passing. He could understand if it hadn't snowed and they were trying to find tracks in the rocks.

"What do you think, Phipps?"

"Don't know, Sir. I just can't understand how we missed them. This many men spread out like we were, you would think someone would have found something."

"I'm thinking we'd better call it off and head back to the fort."

"We can't do that, Sir!" Phipps cried out. "We can't leave Tye out here with that mad man. We...we just can't do that."

"Do you have any idea where they are? If you do or if you have any idea what we can do, I'm open to suggestions. We cannot help Tye if we can't find him." Phipps stared at the Lieutenant, not knowing what to say. "Well?" Paddock said.

"I...I don't know what to do," Phipps whispered.

Paddock looked at the sun. "It will be dark in an hour or so. Make camp and get me a rider that knows the way to Clark."

"Do you have an idea, Sir?"

"I'll send a dispatch to Thurston and tell him the situation and ask for his orders on what to do. How long will it take a rider to reach Clark?"

"Riding hard, he can be there by midnight. Once out of these hills he is no more than ten miles from Clark. I'll get that man, Sir."

Paddock sit down and took out pencil and paper.

Major Thurston:

After locating Garrison and tending to their wounds we took out after Tye. We have lost all traces of tracks of Tye or the outlaw Yancey. We are camped, waiting your orders.

Lieutenant Paddock

The rider, Private Henry Chambers, took the dispatch, an extra horse and headed south, toward Clark. Camp was set for the night.

~~~

Tye held his breath and exhaled slowly as he sighted down the barrel of the Henry. Yancey was riding away from him, maybe two hundred yards below him. It was going to be a very difficult shot in the best of conditions. It was almost dusk which added to the problem. Maybe I can at least hit the horse. He didn't like the idea but he had no choice. It would be a lucky shot. He squeezed the trigger slowly...then released the pressure. If he missed it would only warn Yancey that he was this close and he would make a run for it...a dangerous run for him and Tye chasing him on this snow and ice. I'll make camp and hit him in the morning. Yancey would be making campo also, if he's smart. It's going to be a cold night he thought as he looked up at the clearing sky. He backtracked about a quarter of a mile where he had spotted a small cave in a rock cliff with a stand of oaks around it. The oaks indicated water was there, or at least water is there at times. Maybe this would be one of those times.

Dismounting and walking into the stand of oaks, he was pleased to find a small pool of water. The cave was deeper than he had thought, maybe fifteen feet. 'Sandy will like that,' he thought. He unsaddled Sandy, and led him to the pool to let him drink his fill. When he was through, he gave him the last of the oats. He walked back to the back of the cave, looking at the walls. There were paintings on them...old paintings...pictures of buffalo, wolves, bears, and creatures that he did not recognize but looked to be huge. The ceiling was blackened by many fires of a long time ago. He made a small fire that would be almost invisible from outside the cave. He gathered enough wood for

95

the night. He took out the coffee pot and filled it from the pool. In a few minutes he was drinking hot, strong coffee and chewing jerky.

Walking to the mouth of the cave he sat down Indian style, legs crossed, chewing the jerky and looking toward the west. The air was crisp and clear and one could see a long way. He looked upon an empty land, nothing moving. The animals were holed up and the birds were deep in the trees, huddled together for warmth. Nothing stirred anywhere and it was quiet, very quiet, and pleasant. It was a night that one could forget his troubles…except one that was thinking of Yancey Cates.

Suddenly a slight flicker of light caught Tye's eyes. He blinked and looked again. It was gone. Had he saw it? He wasn't sure. He continued starring and soon saw it again and then a slightly larger fire.

"YANCEY!" he blurted out. "You must be damn cold to chance a fire like that." He figured it to be two, maybe three miles off. He stood up, stretched and walked back to the fire and lay down on his blanket. Sandy nickered and looked at Tye. "You are happy to be here all warm and cozy aren't you boy?" Sandy shook his head and went back to eating what was left of his oats. Tye went to sleep thinking of his warm cozy bed at home and the beautiful lady he could be curled up against.

~~~

Yancey huddled over the small fire. His hands shook as he held the coffee cup to his lips. The hot liquid felt good as he swallowed it. He could not find a good place to camp. He finally settled on camping on the south side of a hill which had very little protection if the wind increased. He was tired, miserable, cold, and wondered why he came to this land that had done nothing except cause him pain; not only physical pain but mental pain. He had lost his brother to the damn bluecoats. He had lost friends who had depended on him to the bluecoats. He almost lost his life by hanging by the bluecoats. And who led the bluecoats…that sonofabitch Watkins.

He lay down and pulled his blankets over him and thought of his past. His parents were very religious, in fact his father preached sometimes at the country Church when the regular pastor was away. Seems every time that Church door was open, him and his brother Billy were there. Their pa did not believe in killing anything unless it was killed to eat. Killing a human was unthinkable to him and ma. Their parents worked hard on the little farm they had and it took its toll on them. They both looked much older than they were. The boys did their share…and hated every minute of it.

When it was apparent there was going to be a war, both boys, despite strong objections from their parents, joined the Confederacy. He didn't keep track of how many Yankees he killed but it was more than he cared to count. Billy had done his share too, and for what? They were both key members of the most famous guerilla fighters in the Confederacy…Quantrill's Raiders. After the war they went home to dead parents and a burned out home; burned by Sherman on his march through the south. They had nothing so they joined Quantrill. They continued their raiding, killing, raping…only thing now it was not soldiers they were killing but civilians. Seems like he had been killing as long as he could remember.

He and Billy knew hard work and knew hunger for it seems there was never enough food on the table at home. It was the same during the war and mostly since. He had never bought into the Christian way of thinking. His parents prayed to God every day and what did it get them…hard work, hunger, and finally murdered. He was eighteen years old and Billy was twenty when they joined the Confederacy. They had known nothing but killing for the last six years. A man gets kinda calloused to it after a while and he certainly had.

He lay there looking at his life. He was twenty-four years old. He had his guns, horses, and essentials, all stolen. The only thing he owned personally was the clothes on his back, except for the coat, it was stolen also.

"Not much to show for twenty-four years of life," he mumbled. For the first time in years, he maybe felt a little regret for the life he had chosen to live. He could read, write and do numbers which is more than seventy percent of the people out here can do. He had the looks to go with his book learning. He could have done something with his life other than what he had done. The outlaw life looked good to him and Billy. Not much work and the pay was going to be good. It hadn't worked out they way. His dreams turned to reality, being on the lam, sleeping in bedrolls on the ground in the rain and cold. Always moving from one place to another and always looking over your shoulder. He had his choices in life and he had made the wrong ones. He realized that now but it was too late to change things.

"DAMN." He shouted in disgust… "Damn." His horses looked at him and then went back to scratching the ice, trying to get to the short grass underneath.

~~~

It was before midnight when Private Chambers crossed the bridge over Los Mora Creek and entered Fort Clark. He told the guard he had an urgent dispatch for Major Thurston. The guard let him pass and he made a bee line for Thurston's quarters. When a weary looking Thurston opened the door, Chambers snapped to attention and saluted which was returned by Thurston.

"What is it, private?"

"A dispatch from Lieutenant Paddock Sir." He handed the note to Thurston who ripped it open and turned to where the light of the lamp was good enough for him to read.

"Wait here, private."

"Yes Sir." Thurston shut the door and scrambled around trying to find his pants and shoes. He didn't bother taking his night shirt off; he threw a coat on and opened the door.

"Let's go to Tye's home." He and the private left, trotting toward Tye's.

"WHO GOES THERE?" a voice from along the bushes that lined Los Moras shouted.

"MAJOR THURSTON."

"Come."

The man stepped out. "Sorry Sir. I didn't recognize you."

"That's exactly what you are supposed to do, private. Good work." He turned and headed to the porch on the house. Stepping on the porch he saw the rifle barrel pointing at him from inside.

"Yu bett'r speek up or yur gonna be full of hols damn quik like." Thurston smiled. He knew that old man would be alert.

"It's me, Buff…Major Thurston." The door opened and he went inside.

"Whut's wrong, Majur?" Buff asked, fearing the worse.

"The patrol lost Tye's trail. They need a tracker, Buff." Buff looked toward the door going to Rebecca's room. Thurston knew what he was thinking. "I will have Rebecca escorted to the O'Malley's. There will be guards posted there. She will be fine."

Yu sure, Majur. I dun give my wurd to Tye tha I wud make shur nuthin happened ta her."

"I guarantee you she will be safe."

"Give me a minite to git my thangs." Buff walked into his room and shut the door. Thurston walked to Rebecca's door and quietly knocked.

"Who is it?"

"Major Thurston, Rebecca. Can you come out please?" She hurried out the door putting her robe on. "Is Tye okay?" she asked, her voice showing a little panic.

"Yes. Yes...as far as we know he's fine."

"Then what is the matter?" Thurston explained the situation to her and she agreed to go to the O'Malley's. "Could I speak to Buff before you leave?"

"Of course." Buff came out of his room in his buckskins, complete with a buffalo robe. "Buff, Rebecca wants to speak to you. We'll step outside and wait."

Rebecca came over to Buff and wrapped her arms around him, kissing him on the cheek. "Buff, you have to find him...please. I'm really scared this time. That man is so awful."

"Rebecca, yu don't fret yourself nun. I'll find tha man uf yurs and then we'll git tha thar Yancey feller. Yu jus go to tha O'Malley's and lay low. Yu'll be fine. He hugged her back and left out the door. Two soldiers stepped inside explaining they were to escort her to the O'Malley's. "Give me a minute," she said.

Outside Thurston explained to Buff that Chambers would take him to the patrol and then it was up to him to find Tye.

Gary McMillan

Chapter Twelve

Dawn broke clear and cold. Tye had eaten his jerky and was already headed toward the hill he had spotted the fire on last night. It was well below freezing last night and the snow had turned to ice. He was moving slow because, not only of the danger of Sandy slipping and breaking a leg, but the sharp edges of the ice when a hoof broke through could cut a horse's fetlocks, crippling him for a few days.

The sun would warm things by midmorning and by noon or shortly after, the snow and ice would be gone. That is the way Texas winters are. The cold spells usually lasted only two or three days then warm weather would set in for a period before the cycle repeated itself.

He knew the camp would be empty before he ever found it. Yancey would be on the move early. He looked at the location of the camp without dismounting. He patted Sandy on the neck, "Old Yancey probably got a little chilly last night, Sandy." He led him to the opposite side of the camp and stopped. Tye kneeled and studied the icy ground. The tracks were plain, and heading slightly southwest. "Let's go, Sandy."

~~~

Yancey was cussing something fierce. His packhorse had slipped and snapped the bone just above the fetlock on his front leg. Yancey dismounted, took out his pistol to put the animal out of his misery then decided against firing a shot. He took his knife and cut the suffering animal's throat. He took just the things he needed from the packs and put them in the saddlebags of his mount. He headed out, walking and leading his horse not wanting to chance it breaking a leg also. Left on foot, without a horse, he was a dead man for sure. 'Hell, I probably am anyway,' he thought. He had headed southwest hoping to get out of these damn hills. He wanted to be where he could see a long ways…behind him mostly, to see who is coming.

Shortly after noon he could see the open country before him. His spirits lifted some by the sight. He mounted his horse and galloped for the first time in days. The snow and ice was gone. He was leaving tracks but at least he could now see Tye and could set up a surprise for him. He knew he was coming and soon it would be over…one of them would be dead.

~~~

"Damn, you made good time, Chambers," Phipps said as Buff and Chambers rode in just as the sun was breaking the rim of the hills.

"Howdy, Buff."

"Got any coffee?" Chambers asked. "Been a long night." Paddock came over and told Chambers he did a great job. He walked over to Buff and introduced himself.

"We need someone to find Tye's tracks, Buff. Evidently, Thurston thinks you are the man for the job."

"If he didn't fly, I'll find him," Buff said. He turned to Phipps. "Where did you lose him?"

"Come on, I'll show you."They rode off together. They pulled up where the men had stopped looking last night.

"Right here is where we stopped looking…just gave up." Buff sat on his horse, looking in the distance. To the northwest was steep hills. 'No way would a man go that way in this ice and snow,' he thought to himself. Due west looked to be more of the same. To the southwest was also steep hills, but there was something else. It looked like a gap between the hills with steep walls. 'If I was here yesterday and looking for a place to hole up, it would be there.'

"See tha kut between thos hills yonder," he said to Phipps, pointing with his rifle.

"Yes Sir. I see it."

"Go get the patrol and meet me there," Buff said riding off. Phipps watched him go and wondered what the hell he wanted to go there for. He left to get Paddock and the patrol.

"You mean he has already found the trail?" A skeptical Paddock asked.

"Don't know, Sir. But he told me to take you to that cut... there," Phipps said pointing. They rode out, neither saying anything, both wondering. When they arrived at the cut, there was Buff, sitting by the fire that Tye had left smoldering. Phipps and Paddock looked at each other in disbelief.

Paddock looked at Buff. "How in all that's holy, did you know?"

"Been trackin all my life, Lootenant. Don't take no genus ta reed a trac on tha ground. It taks sum practice ta figure out whut tha man wud do tha yur following if you lost the trail. Lerned a long time ago ta put myself in their plac and see whut I wud do. If yu had tuk tha time to luk at the lay uf tha land whare Tye wus headed, yu wud have seed that tha only smart way ta go, wus this heer cut. Tha uther directions wur steep hills...no plac ta go in ice if'n wun is smart. Tye's smart." Phipps and Paddock looked at each other ... both feeling pretty damn stupid.

"Man or beest, both gonna fin a plac ta hole up in bad wether. Member tha Phipps. Follur tha tracs and if yu luse them, luk around, see whu yu wud do. Be suprized how often yu ar rite."

"I'll remember," Phipps promised and walked off to tend to his horse while the Lieutenant and Buff discussed the situation.

"How far behind are we?" Paddock questioned. Buff looked to the southwest where Tye had headed and spit a wad of tobacco before answering.

"Most fore hours...problee kloser ta three." Paddock looked in the direction Buff was looking.

"With the snow and ice covering everything last night before Tye camped, why do you think he headed there," nodding to where they were both looking. "Do you think he found tracks this morning after the snow?"

"Kudn't say fur shur, Lootenant. I thank he did wun uf too thangs. Ether he jus took a chance tha Yancey went tha way, or he knu fur shur. Maybee he smelled smoke fum tha breeze last nite. It wus frum tha direction yu kno. Maybee he jus saw a fire on a hill an figured it wus Yancey. Kud be a lot uf thangs, but I feel he's got a handle on tha situation and kno whut he's doing."

Paddock snickered, "From the stories I have heard about him, I figure you're right. He knows where he is going and what he's doing. From what I have heard about you, you're pretty well known also.

That little feat this morning was amazing and I don't mind telling you, I felt pretty dumb. I've got a lot to learn out here."

"Thar's kno need ta feel dumb, Lootenant. All uf us wure a greener at wun time or anuther. Man's always leerning thangs out heer and beleeve me, thar is a lot ta leern." He looked at Paddock and knew what he was fixing to ask. "A greener is a man whu knos nuthin abut nuthin" He slapped his thigh and laughed heartily. Paddock looked at him for a moment, then laughed also.

Paddock walked over to the tracks Tye left. "Even I could follow them," he said turning back, looking at Buff and smiling.

"Yep, even a greener kud. Thar's wun more trick though, Lootenant."

"What's that?"

"Being able to tell if yur minites behind or hours behind. If yur minites behind and jus follering tracs, yu kud stumble on tha person yur ar follering axcidently and git yur butt blowed off. Tric ta reeding sign is mor'n jus follering tracs: man needs ta kno how manee men he's follering: needs ta kno how thar heeled. Tha's fronteer talk fur how tha ar armed, Lootenant," Buff said smiling. "A gud tracker can leern ta tell wun hosses huffprint frum anuther as eezy as knoing wun man's face frum anuther man. An Injun kan cum into a white mans kamp and kno how manee men wur thar, how manee hosses tha had, whut they ate, and when tha left.

Paddock shook his head. He now knew why Thurston and Garrison told him to listen to these men. He intended to corner Buff and Tye and just listen to them like a school kid does his teacher. He laughed at a thought he just had; 'me, a graduate of West Point and a student to men who never sat in a classroom.' He laughed again.

Phipps came up at that time. "Don't you think we need to get after Tye, Sir?"

"Yes we do., Corporal. I've been thinking about being in a classroom and lost track of time. Get the men mounted and let's go."

"Yes Sir." Phipps turned and walked away toward the men, then stopped and looked back at the Lieutenant. "A classroom?" he said scratching the back of his neck.

~~~

By midmorning the snow and ice was beginning to disappear making Yancey's tracks easy to follow on the damp ground. Tye was in the low foothills now and up ahead was gently rolling hills with a few gullies. A man could see a long ways here with nothing but low sage, cactus, and chaparral springing up from the rocky ground. Tye stood in the stirrups looking southwest where the tracks were heading hoping to get a glimpse of Yancey.

"He's moving pretty fast Sandy," Tye said looking at the stride of Yancey's horse. He kicked Sandy in the flanks and set out at a gallop, keeping one eye on the tracks and one eye on the lookout for trouble. After covering about four miles, he reined Sandy up sharply. The tracks veered left heading southeast...directly toward Brackett, Fort Clark...and Rebecca. A chilling cold settled in the pit of his stomach at what could happen. He had never before felt fear like this. He kicked Sandy into an all out run, trying to close the distance. The fear slowly turned to rage, a rage like he never felt before. A rage so strong he lost all thoughts of his surroundings. The landscape was just a blur to him, his eyes focusing on nothing, his mind blocking out all thoughts... except of Rebecca. God he loved her and he was tired of the game with this sonofabitch. He was going to kill him on sight, no thought, no remorse...just kill him.

The rage that had built up in his guts slowly faded, replaced by common sense and he knew he was pushing Sandy too hard. He pulled him up, dismounted and looked at the tracks. They were still headed toward Clark but the tracks showed the horse was tiring. He remounted and followed at a trot, giving Sandy a chance to recover his strength. A mile later they hit the Mail Road, a few miles west of Clark. Like Tye figured, Yancey followed the road, his tracks mingling with others traveling the road. Tye could still follow but it was slow going having to find the print with the cracked shoe among all the others on the road.

He walked, leading Sandy looking at the tracks. This was a waste of time he figured. It was only letting the man get farther away, closer to Rebecca. He mounted Sandy and moved to the north side of the road and set out at a trot. He watched the ground for any tracks leaving the road. If he doesn't find them, then Yancey's either going to actually go to Clark or he is headed south. There was still three hours of daylight left. He didn't figure Yancey would show his face there in the daylight so he slowed Sandy to a walk. He stayed on the north side of the road till he could see Clark in the distance, crossed over the road and headed away from Clark, staying on the south side, looking for tracks headed south.

~~~

Paddock was impressed by this old man tracking Tye. He figured from watching the way he moved, the way he talked, and way he rode, Phipps was right: this is one old man that could still be hell on wheels in a fight. He pictured him forty or fifty years ago fighting Indians and dealing with every other hardship the land of the Rockies offered to those trappers back then. He didn't know much about them except what he had read in the novels and a little history of them at the Point. He figured they were all like this man, tougher than nails. He never figured to actually meet one of these men and certainly not one he had read about. He would love to sit around a listen to his stories.

He saw Buff waiting for them about a quarter mile away. He wondered what the problem was as there was still some daylight left. Arriving he asked, "Is there a problem, Buff?"

"Yancey's and Tye's tracs jus turned south. I don't kno this land very well but I figured tha Fort Clark is in tha direcshun."

Paddock turned in the saddle and looked at Phipps who was behind him with Sergeant Baker. Phipps nodded that Buff was right.

"Damn," Paddock uttered under his breath. "Damn."

"Thar's sum trees yonder," Buff said pointing with his rifle. "Problee sum water and grass fur tha horses. Only a hour uf daylite left, Lootenant. Whut abut making kamp?"

Paddock again turned in the saddle and told Baker we will camp over there where those trees are. Arriving at the place, there was a couple of large oaks and some smaller pecan trees. There was a rock basin that had water in it. The men filled their canteens and coffee pots before letting the horses come in to drink. Soon, there was the wonderful smell of coffee, bacon frying, and the raucous laughter of hard men; men that rode this country protecting the settlers, risking their life for thirteen dollars a month: men that for the most part had no family other than their fellow troopers; men who lived their lives at a secluded fort with no comforts of the big cities. This is the life of a

United States Cavalryman and there wasn't much glamour in it. Coffee, hot bacon and greasy biscuits wasn't much of a meal to most folks, but to a soldier, it was a real treat when on patrol.

~~~

About three miles from the fort, Tye found the tracks of Yancey's horse. He was headed due south. He checked the sun and figured he had about thirty minutes of light left. The tracks showed Yancey was trotting his horse. The tracks were plain, maybe an hour or so old and easy to follow. Tye had Sandy at a gallop, hoping to make up ground on the outlaw. He was thankful for the moisture that had fallen, otherwise he would be walking, following the tracks on foot, looking for chipped or turned over rocks on the rocky ground.

It was now becoming dark and he figured he was too close to risk going any farther and stumbling into Yancey. He found a spot that was in the back of a thick stand of mesquite that had a small clearing in the center. He watered Sandy, hobbled him and then unrolled his bedroll on the ground. There was enough of the short grammar grass for Sandy. The grass was brown and not very nourishing but was better than not eating. Tye made a cold camp and sat on his bedroll chewing jerky and sipping water from his canteen before lying down. He was almost asleep when a coyote howled that was so close, Tye thought he was in camp. Even Sandy was excited, stomping his hooves and snorting. Tye sat there for a full five minutes before lying back down. He knew a man could not sneak in on him as thick as the mesquite was and besides, Sandy was the best sentry a man could have.

~~~

Yancey had made a cold camp also. He didn't think Watkins was close to him because he felt he had covered his tracks by staying on the Old Mail Road, mixing his tracks with others. He decided on a cold camp just to be on the safe side. He figured he was about four, maybe five miles from the southwest corner of Clark. Before daylight he would find where Los Moras flowed out of Clark on its way to the Rio Grande. He had heard that Tye's house was along the creek so he figured he could find it. He went to sleep smiling, thinking of Tye's wife and what he was going to do to her.

~~~

Buff found him the center of attention in the camp. All these men had heard stories or read, the ones who could read, about Shakespeare and men like him. As usual, most of the questions were about Bridger. Buff was used to that. Lieutenant Paddock asked Buff to give a synopsis of what the life of a mountain man was like.

"A whut?" Buff asked. Ninety nine percent of the others was wondering what the hell the Lieutenant was wanting also.

"You know...what it was like back then. A condensed version of what was the daily life like," Paddock explained.

"That may take awhile," Buff said. "Can I have some more coffee?" One of the men returned with the pot and emptied it filling Buff's and the others' cups. Everyone got comfortable and all talking ceased.

"Has aneewun uf yu been tat ha Rockies?" No one said anything. "Wal, tha are God's masterpeece. If'n anee wun uf yu wure ever thar, yu wud kno thar had ta be a God ta make anee thang tha purty. Tha tops uf thos montons teched tha sky. Manee times, tha klouds wure below tha tops. Hell, manee a time, I was on tha side of them montons luking down on tha clouds or maybe surrounded by them. When tha happened, yu kudn't see fur and it wus kooler and always mistee. Tha trees stopped growing on manee uf them tha wure so high." He took a sip of the coffee and leaned back against a large rock.

"Tha eerly years uf tha beever trade wus easy. Onliest thang wun had ta wurry about was starvin, freezin, or gitten eaten by tha kritters. Yu had pacs of wolves, yu had panthers, and tha wurst uf all, tha grizz. In lean yeers, the grizz wuld stalk a man and try ta make a meal uf him. A full growed grizz may stan up ta ten fut and way over a thousand pounds a tha wurst dispostshun yu ever did see. Tha Injuns wure purty friendly thos ferst yeers. In abut '26 thangs changed. Tha wuz tha yeer Tye's pa and me became frends. Tha Blackfut wure tired uf more and more us us trappr's kumning into their land, takin game tha needed. After tha yeer, yu kud die frum freezin, starving, tha kritters, or git yuself scalped by tha Blacfut."

"Was the Blackfoot as bad as the Apache?" a trooper asked.

"Don't kno these heer Apache too well. I figure tha ar like tha uther tribes tha hate tha white man and are hell on wheels in a fite and meener than wun wud ever thank. Bac then, the Blacfut mostly had bows, no guns. Thaw wus our onlee advantage but then agan, a gud Blacfut warrur kud shut ten or mor arrors a minute and at seventy yards or less, abut as accurate as a man with a rifle. Wun did't wunt ta be by his lonsum in them montons, I'll tale yu that."

"Tha daly life uf a trappr wus pretee much tha same day after day. Up at daylite, run and bait traps and kum bac fur breakfast. A little aftur noon, tha traps wure run again and rebated. If'n yu had beever, you wud spend tha rest uf tha day skinnin the beever and fleshin tha plews. Befo yu ask, plews ar tha beever skins an fleshin is scraping all tha fat off them. It's a lot uf work ta git them to whare they will kure out soft. When tha beever played out, yu wuld move to anuther creek." He finished his coffee and added, "These ole bones need sum rest so I'll see ya boys befo daylite."

109

Gary McMillan

Chapter Thirteen

Well before the eastern sky was turning grey, Tye had broke camp and was leading Sandy out of the mesquite thicket. When out, he toed the stirrup, swung his leg over and settled his butt in the saddle. He checked his Henry for the second time to make sure everything was okay and rested the butt on his right thigh, his right hand gripping the rifle. He was ready if trouble came. He knew that Yancey's camp had to be close so he walked Sandy slowly, trying to keep as quite as possible. It was nerve-racking work, expecting a bullet at any time. He walked Sandy about a mile when he figured he had pushed his luck long enough.

He dismounted, tied Sandy to a sage, and continued on foot. His moccasin boots helped in times like this. Placing each foot carefully before putting his full weight down, he could feel a twig or limb before his weight snapped it. It was eerie it was so quite. Moving on silent feet the only sound was an occasional mesquite or sage limb scraping against his pants and it was only a whisper. He knew he was close, he could feel it. He held the Henry in his left hand, his navy colt in the right, cocked and ready to fire.

Suddenly he stopped, standing perfectly still. He thought he heard a horse blow. Standing there unmoving, he strained his ears for any sound, his eyes trying to pierce the blackness before dawn. He slowly knelt to the ground, making no sudden movements that could give him away. He stayed there until the ache in his knees forced him to stand. He stood slowly and was almost full up right when he saw the flash of a rifle, the slug knocking his hat off his head before he heard the report of the fired gun. He fell to the ground and fired two quick rounds at where the flash was. Yancey fired again and splinters from a mesquite limb stung Tye's face. "Bastard must be able to see in the dark like a damn cat," Tye mumbled to himself. He rolled to his left and waited. Five minutes went by, then ten. He still waited because in a situation like this, the man who moves first usually gets himself killed. He was still waiting when the sky started to lighten some, allowing him to see a little better. He searched the crest of the hill, every bush and every rock that he could see.

He was still lying there when he heard the horse, running away from him. "Dammitt," he hollered and ran to the top of the hill. He could see Yancey thru the early morning light but he was moving fast and was over a hundred yards away. Tye quickly holstered his colt and raised his Henry to his shoulder. He aimed a little ahead of Yancey and squeezed the trigger. He quickly fired again and then again. He knew he had missed with all three shots. He was over a quarter mile from where he left Sandy. Tye set out at a dead run to get back to him.

~~~

Yancey could not believe he missed with his first shot. He had the damn scout dead in his sights. 'Musta been the low light,' he figured. It was now kill or be killed and he figured it would end today, tomorrow at the latest. He had planned to leave early to get to the fort, but he was so tired he over slept. His horse blowing had woke him up and warned him someone was near. He reached down and patted the horse on the neck. "Thanks old boy." He had reined in and now held the horse to a trot. He glanced over his shoulder but saw nothing. He was heading south, away from the fort. .He wanted this to be one on one between him and Watkins, not with a whole damn fort of blue bellies. He was searching the terrain ahead, trying to spot a good place to wait for him. He wouldn't miss this pain in the ass again; this so called bigger than life man named Watkins.

~~~

Buff was leading the patrol down the Old Mail Road toward Clark just as it was starting to get light. He didn't figure Yancey would go to the fort or Brackett so he was on the north side following Tye's tracks and Phipps was on the south side looking where they left the road. Phipps suddenly pulled up and whistled. Buff kicked his horse and rode over to him quick like. They both dismounted. Buff kneeled down studied the tracks. "Thar's tha kracked shoe," he said pointing to it. "Good job, Phipps." He stood up and was looking in the direction of the tracks when they both heard what sounded like shots. "Did yu heer tha?" Buff asked.

"Yes sir, sounded like three or four shots." The patrol was still a quarter of a mile behind them.

"I'm gonna hed toward thos shots. Yu wait heer and bring tha patrol quick." He kicked his horse in the flanks and headed south at a full gallop. He only checked the ground every once in awhile for tracks. The ground here was damp and not near as rocky as in the hills so there was no way to hide one's tracks, especially if you were in a hurry.

The patrol arrived where Phipps was waiting.

"Where's Buff headed?' Paddock asked as he reined in his mount.

"Found tracks headed south then we heard shots. Buff headed toward them and told me to fetch you there quick."

"Let's go then." He turned in the saddle and pumped his arm twice. "AT A GALLOP," he ordered and the patrol was off quickly, following Phipps.

About a half mile ahead of the patrol, Buff was dismounting. Tye had backtracked to this spot. He leaned over in the saddle and studied the tracks some more. He nodded his head and looked into the mesquite thicket and smiled. "Tha thar boy knos his business," he muttered. He figured Tye had saw this spot when he passed earlier and when it was almost dark, he came back here to camp.

He could see the patrol coming and decided to wait for them. Phipps arrived first just ahead of Paddock and the patrol.

"Tye passed this spot then kame bac heer ta kamp in tha thar stand uf mesqueets over thar." He nodded toward the mesquites.

"Why would he go by them and come back?" Paddock asked.

"He kno's tha thar Yancey feller is aming to kill him. A stand like tha is hard fur a man to get thru without makin sum noise, specially if'n yur trying it at nite. He picked a gud plac to kamp." He mounted his horse and pointed south. "Thar still heeded due south so let's go." They had been trotting for five minutes or so when Buff threw up his hand, stopping the patrol. He dismounted and was studying the ground when the patrol came up to him. "STAY BAC,' he shouted at the patrol. They stopped so quick some of the horses ran into the rears of the horse in front. He studied the ground some more then walked over to Lieutenant Paddock. "Tye tied Sandy up to tha sage over thar," he

113

said nodding in the direction of a large sage bush. "He musta kno'd he wus klose ta Yancey's kamp. He left here," pointing to the ground, "on foot. Gonna be slow trackin frum here on." He turned and followed Tye's faint tracks. Moccasin's leave a lot less of a print than a leather soled boot.

McClellan turned to Sergeant Baker. "Sergeant, hold the men back for a few minutes, then come at a walk." He handed his reins to the man next to Sergeant Baker. He and Phipps followed a few steps behind Buff. They could see nothing even close to a track, yet the old mountain man seemed to know where he was going. Buff suddenly stopped, studying the ground all around him.

"What is it?" Phipps asked.

Buff spit a wad of tobacco on the ground. 'Tye got hiself shot at here." He pointed to a sage. "He dropp'd behind tha bush and I figure he knew tha sage wusn't gonna stop bullets so he rolled ove'r thar, behind that rock jus as the next shots cum thru the ferst bush he wus behind." He showed them the splintered limb. Phipps and Paddock looked at each other, both smiling and shaking their heads. Paddock stood back up, and looking back at the patrol, pumped his arm twice, signaling them to come in a hurry. Buff had walked to the top of the hill and found the shell cases where Yancey had fired at Tye. Looking back to where Paddock stood, he couldn't believe he missed. He found where Tye had fired also. Walking down into the camp he spotted Yancey's horse's tracks, leaving in a hurry. Walking a little to the left of them, he found Sandy's tracks. From the distance between the tracks, he was at a gallop also.

He walked back to the spot where the shell cases were and motioned for them to come to him. Arriving there, they kneeled down where Buff was sitting, legs crossed, Indian style. Buff handed the shell casings to the captain. "Yancey wus heer, behind tha sage when he fired at Tye." Both men looked at where Tye had been.

"How in hell did he miss?" Phipps questioned.

"Had ta be low lite," Buff answered. "Shuting can be tricky in thos conditions." He stood up as did McClellan and Phipps. "Went down ta Yancey's kamp. Yancey lit a shuck south and Tye is chasing him in a hurry."

The patrol arrived and the three mounted their horses. "Let's get after them," McClellan ordered. He raised his arm and pumped it.

Once again they were following Buff who was already two hundred yards away. McClellan was impressed with this little old man. Not only was he a hell of a tracker, but he seemed to be more at home in a saddle than he or his men were. He had been a little leery of the stories that Buff had been telling...but no more. He figured Buff was down playing his role as a mountain man and he was probably as good as or better than one would think from listening to him talk. Yep, that old man was tougher than nails.

Gary McMillan

Chapter Fourteen

Tye was becoming a little nervous. Looking back to the north over his shoulder, he could see another storm coming. With the temperature it would probably be just a cold rain, maybe a little snow. Either way, if he didn't catch up with Yancey today, the storm could wipe out any trace of Yancey. He wasn't gaining on the running man like he figured he would. The horse Yancey had was still running good, showing no signs of tiring. Sandy wanted to run but Tye held him to an easy lope. He learned a long time ago that running a horse to the point of floundering could get a man killed if he suddenly needed speed. It was just plain stupid to run a horse all out unless it was necessary. Looking back at the storm he wanted to let Sandy loose, let him run to gain some ground, but put down the urge to do so.

The terrain here was gently rolling hills, unlike the steep hills and canyons of yesterday. Here, cactus, mesquite, purple sage and short, sparse grass covered the land instead of huge boulders, cedars, and oaks. The chance of a man being able to hide well enough to ambush another was also less here. Tye figured he had let Sandy run enough, he reined him in and dismounted. He loosened the girth on the saddle to let him breath better. He stood beside Sandy with his arm under his neck, scratching him on the lower jaw on the opposite side while starring in the direction Yancey was running. He wondered how much longer the horse Yancey was riding could hold the pace. Yancey's horse had been loping for a little over two hours now and that was pushing any horse.

Tye reached into his saddlebag and pulled out some jerky. Biting off a piece, he slowly chewed it while pouring some water in his hat and giving Sandy a drink.

"That's a pretty good horse old Yancey has Sandy," Tye said, scratching Sandy between the ears. Sandy nickered and shook his head. "I know," Tye said laughing, "he's not the horse you are."

117

Sandy nodded his head and Tye laughed again. He talked a lot to him when he was on scout. Scouting was a lonely job most of the time and he knew other men out here that talked to their horses a lot also. Sandy had saved his bacon more than once since Major Thurston had given him to Tye after he brought in the Vasquez gang. Buck, Tye's horse at the time had been shot and killed during an ambush. Since that time, Tye and Sandy had been on many patrols and made a good team. Sandy was the best horse he had ever had and he loved him more than anything...well almost more... as he thought of Rebecca. He smiled. She would have my hide if she thought her and Sandy were in a close race like that. He took another bite of the jerky and put the rest back in his saddlebag. He tightened the girth, toed the stirrup and mounted up. Tye clucked and lightly kicked Sandy in the flanks and they were back on the trail.

~~~

Yancey saw the storm coming and unlike Tye, he was happier than a pig eating slop. He knew if he stayed ahead of Watkins, the storm would wipe out his tracks and freeing him to make plans. He had slowed his horse to a walk, allowing him to blow some. He had no water to spare to give his horse so he was desperately trying to find some. He knew horses and knew he was pushing this one to the limit. He finally decided to pull up, dismounted and tied his horse to a sage bush that had some short grama grass around it. He walked to the crest of a nearby hill and dropped to a crouch when he reached the top, not wanting to skyline himself. He sat down, made himself comfortable and studied his back trail.

"Damn!" he swore under his breath. Two miles or so back, he saw a rider coming. He watched for a full minute. "That's Watkins," he said to himself. 'Maybe he is part Apache like people say,' he thought to himself. 'I know for damn sure, he's part bloodhound. I would have lost most men a couple days ago with the tracks on the road and then the goat tracks. The rest would have quit when the snow fell, but not Watkins. He's becoming a real pain in the ass.'

He backed down the hill and remounted his horse. He checked the sky and figured he had to stay ahead for at least a couple more hours then the storm would be wiping everything out. Maybe he could rest and sort things out then. He had food for two or three more days if he was careful. What he needed now was water, especially for his horse and a good place to hole up to wait out the storm.

~~~

Buff also knew they were in for a storm and pretty damn quick. It didn't take a genius to figure that out. Like Tye and Yancey, he was looking for a place he and the patrol could wait it out. He also knew that after the storm, their finding Tye's tracks would be slim to none. He figured they were about two hours, no more than three behind. From studying both sets of tracks, he figured Tye was less than an hour behind Yancey.

Paddock rode up to him looking at the clouds moving in. He reined in and looked at Buff.

"How do we stand as far as catching up with Tye?"

"Wal. If'n yur talking abut time…two, mabee three hours. If'n yur askin when we will katch up…tha anser is we won't."

Paddock looked at him. "What do you mean by that?"

"Tha thar storm is muvin in purty quik. If it is hav as bad as I thank it is, thar won't be no traks to follur an it's a big kuntry out thar."

"What are you saying, Buff?"

"Kum morning, Tye an tha Yancey feller mite as wal be on tha moon. If tha storm kumin in is as bad as I thank it is, thar won't be a chanc in hell uf finding traks. I thank our mane concern rite now is finding a place fur us to try an sta dry."

"I think you may be right," Paddock replied looking up again at the darkening sky. "See if you can find us a place, Buff." Buff kicked his mount and left in a cloud of dust.

"Where's Buff going Lieutenant?" Phipps asked moving his mount in beside Paddock.

"Looking for us a place to hole up and ride out the storm." Phipps turned and looked up at the sky. "The men had been watching it too. There's going to be hell to pay before dark." Paddock placed his hands on the pommel of his saddle and standing in the stirrups, raised his butt off the saddle a couple inches. It felt great but he knew they had better leave in a hurry to stay up with that old man. Phipps led the patrol out, following Buff.

119

~~~

Tye was keeping one eye on Yancey's tracks and the other on possible ambush sites. In between, he was watching the storm coming in and cursing his luck.

"It's going to be a cold, miserable night, Sandy," he grumbled. Worse than that, he thought, was the fact that Yancey was probably going to be running free, killing, raping, and stealing again after his tracks are wiped out. He didn't relish the idea of having to look over his shoulder, wondering where the cutthroat was. Usually, it was the other way around with the other man looking over his shoulder for Tye.

The terrain here was a little different than it was a couple miles back. The rolling hills had become a little more rugged with steeper hills, gullies, and in places, extremely large boulders. All these were good places for a man to hide. Ahead, about a half mile was a high hill that looked to have very steep sides. 'Maybe there will be a place there to stay dry,' he thought and kicked Sandy into a trot.

He suddenly reined Sandy up. "What the hell?" he burst out. Crossing Yancey's trail was about fifteen horses...unshod horses. Tye dismounted for a closer look

"NASAY," he spit out angrily. He recognized the track of one of the ponies as belonging to the Apache's pony. The pony's right front hoof had two distinct notches on it. Nasay had killed several soldiers and part of Yancey's gang about a month ago. All the Apaches had been killed except for three. 'One of those just had to be him,' Tye thought... 'Damn.' He was in a real quandary now. The Apache tracks were less than an hour old. He walked in a circle and stopped again. Three ponies had left the group, following Yancey. He figured on that because no Apache would have missed the tracks of Yancey's horse and no Apache was going to pass up the opportunity to kill a white man.

Tye squatted down on his heels and tried to reason things out. He wanted Yancey bad but as bad as Yancey was, the fifteen braves could do a lot more damage. He decided he would find a place to hole up and in the morning make a wide circle and try to pick up the Apache tracks. He knew they would hole up too as would Yancey. He smiled as a thought came to him. 'Here we are three different groups, all looking for someone to capture or kill and we are probably going to be camped within a mile or so of each other and not know it.' He shook his head and smiled again at the situation.

"There's what we're looking for, Sandy," he whispered, patting his horse on the neck. He dismounted and looked the place over; a depression in the side of the hill and two large, heavy branched cedars on the top, leaning away from the slope of the hill.

"Unless it comes a real gully washer, Sandy, we might just stay half dry." He gave Sandy a drink from his hat and then began gathering wood. He figured a small fire against the back wall would be virtually invisible during the storm and would certainly be a comfort to him. Coffee, hot bacon and a greasy biscuit sounded damn good. He took his slicker out and hung it on a low limb of one of the cedars so it would be handy. He leaned his rifle against the back wall also. He piled some rocks in a small circle to surround the fire and made himself comfortable. A minute later, the first cold drops begin to fall. Being camped on this hill, he was higher than most of the surrounding land and he could see a gray wall of heavy rain moving toward him from the northwest. He put his slicker on, pulled his hat down over his face, and squatted against the back wall close to the fire.

~~~

Two miles north of Tye's camp, the patrol was being pounded by the storm. The only place they could find was in a thick stand of mesquite and cedar; which was not much protection against the driving rain and wind. With the temperature in the mid forties, the troopers were not only wet, but cold also. There was little talk as the men sat with their knees pulled up to their chest, their hats pulled down low to keep the water from running down their collars. The horses were miserable also standing with their heads down, shoulder muscles shivering. It was only mid afternoon but with the heavy clouds, one would think it was dusk. It had been a miserable thirty minutes since the rain began.

Buff sat next to Paddock and Phipps. He raised the brim of his hat and took a look at the sky. He was surprised to see patches of blue sky back to the north. In the next minute, the rain slacked up to only a drizzle. Men stood up cursing, stretching cramped legs and shaking the

121

water off their slickers and hats. Buff knew just how old he was when he tried to stand up. It took him a few seconds to stand straight.

"Check your weapons and then wipe them down," Sergeant Baker ordered. One of the troopers, a new recruit, was grumbling and complaining about the order. Baker grabbed him by the collar and jerked the startled private's face up, their noses almost touching.

"You say one more damn word I'll whip you within an inch of your life. Now quit your bellyaching and do what I said." He threw the man down on his butt. The private stood back up and began cleaning his rifle and colt.

Corporal Phipps walked over to the private when Baker walked away. "Don't ever question an order out here private. Baker is tough and he meant what he said about whipping you. You wouldn't be the first to feel his wrath. You do what he tells you, stick close to him when things get tough and you just might live long enough to celebrate your first anniversary of being stationed at Clark when it comes around."

Buff was folding up his slicker when Paddock walked over. Buff looked up at him.

"We still have sum daylite left, Lootenant. We kan git a little kloser ta Tye if we git started."

Paddock looked at where Tye's tracks were before the rain and saw no trace of them now. "Do you have any idea where he is?"

"Don't know exactly but I can find him."

"BAKER," Paddock hollered.

"Yes Sir."

"Get the Men mounted. We're moving out."

"Yes Sir."

Buff was already out in front, anxious to find some trace of Tye.

~~~

Yancey had his left hand on the pommel of his saddle preparing to mount, when he suddenly stopped, feeling something or someone was behind him. He slowly turned his head to look. A cold, icy feeling went through him. Three Apache warriors stood not thirty feet away, each with a rifle pointed directly at him. He could go for his gun but knew he was dead if he tried. He didn't want to surrender either and face a terrible death at the hand of these savages. He had heard stories about what they do to a prisoner and he sure as hell did not want to find out if they were true or not.

He kept his back to them and raised his hands. He knew he was a dead man but he was going to take one or two with him. One of the braves, moving on silent feet, closed the distance while Yancey was trying to decide what to do. Yancey suddenly spun around, intending to dive to the side while pulling his gun. He never got the chance as the closest brave struck him above the ear with the butt of his Sharps and Yancey crumbled to the ground... out cold.

The Apache braves quickly tied Yancey's hands behind his back with rawhide strips and then sat down. After a moment, one got up and walked over to the white man's horse and raised the flap on the saddle bags. Reaching in, he found several strips of jerky. Walking back to the others, he pitched some to each one. He sat down with the other two and chewing their jerky, waited for the white man to wake up so they could have some fun...Apache style.

~~~

Tye was surprised when he saw the tracks. Not so much surprised that they were there because he knew three braves had left the main bunch, but the fact they were so fresh. The tracks had not even filled with water from the soggy ground. Tye dismounted for a closer look and immediately stood up and took his Henry from the saddle scabbard.

"Sandy, those tracks aren't more than five maybe ten minutes old," he whispered. He placed his hand on Sandy's nose, hoping to keep him from whinnying or snorting. He led Sandy back fifty or so yards to a stand of mesquite. He gave him a drink from his hat and left on foot to follow the tracks. From where he was a few minutes ago, he could see the tracks disappearing over a small rise. Almost to the top of the rise, he dropped to the ground when he heard a horse snort. Scooting on his belly, he slipped behind some cedars and looked down the slope. "Damn," he swore. Below him, maybe forty yards was Yancey... and the three Apache. He knew Yancey was still alive because he lay with his hands tied behind him. 'Looks like old Yancey is gonna get what he deserves and then some... and there's nothing wrong with that.' He began to back down the hill. Reaching the bottom he headed for the mesquite where Sandy was. He looked over his shoulder a couple times, making sure the Apache's were not coming over the rise.

Reaching Sandy, he placed the Henry in the scabbard, toed the stirrup and started to mount, but stopped before his leg swung over the saddle. Both feet back on the ground, he placed his arm on the saddle and laid his head on his arm...

"I can't believe this, Sandy. I just can't let a man, even a worthless piece of dung like Yancey; go through what he is fixing to go through." He re-tied Sandy, took the Henry back out and just as he took the first step, he heard the scream. "Damn you Yancey...damn you to hell" he swore as he hurried up the slope. Before he reached the top, he dropped to the ground again.

Yancey was lying on his back, his arms being held by two braves. His shirt was ripped open and the third brave straddled his stomach, waving his Bowie in Yancey's face. All three were laughing. Tye could see where a strip of skin had been pulled from Yancey's chest. He knew Yancey's screaming was only going to make things worse. If there's one thing an Apache can't stand, it's a coward...or a man who screamed and whimpered like some squaw.

Tye was thankful he had the thirteen shot Henry instead of his single shot Sharps. The Henry gave him a chance to get all three but he knew that with the first shot, the two left would disappear like magic. He might accidentally get two, but no way all three. He sighted down the barrel of the rifle and had the vee of the front sight on the chest of the brave that straddled Yancey. He held the sights on the brave and started to squeeze the trigger, but decided to wait a moment to see what was going to happen.

Chapter Fifteen

Buff jerked his mount to a halt. "Whut tha hell!" He dismounted to take a closer look at the tracks. The patrol arrived and he motioned for them to stay back. Paddock and Phipps dismounted and walked to where Buff kneeled.

"What is it, Buff?" Paddock questioned.

"Injuns. Several uf them frum tha luks uf tha traks."

"INDIANS," Paddock cried out excitedly. "Are you sure?"

"Unless yu kno sum white men tha don't shu their hosse's."

Paddock stood by watching Buff read the tracks like he would read a book. Buff stood up and pointed to the mess of tracks.

"Tye cum by heer jus after tha Injuns. Tha Apache saw that Yancey fellers traks and three uf them tuk out after him." He showed them the tracks. "This heer is Yancey's, these are tha Injuns, and this wun set heer is Tye's. Gess these heer Apache are like uther Injuns. Tha jus won't pass up a chance ta kill a white man."

"The Apache is the most ruthless, hellish, sadistic human God ever created." Phipps said. "They are also the best fighting men there is. A warrior will never show fear, will never back down from a fight, and is a master of hit and run...now you see them and now you don't. A general, I forget his name, once said if they had been as numerous as the Comanche or Sioux, Texas would still belong to them. On the other hand, according to Tye, they will never tell a lie, they would never steal from one another and they are loving parents, very gentle with their children."

Sergeant Baker walked up behind Phipps. "I swear, Phipps, that is the most words you have ever said at one time since I knowed you. I'm impressed." Phipps just smiled and walked back to get his and the Lieutenant's horses.

"Wal Lootenant, yu hav a decision ta make. Do yu go after tha Injuns or sta on Tye's and Yancey's traks?"

Paddock squatted down on his heels, pushed his hat back, and sighed. His orders were to find Tye and apprehend Yancey. But then, when the order was given, no one knew about any Apache bucks running loose. Those Apache could do more damage than one man could…even a man like Yancey.

Buff could see the young officer wasn't sure what to do. "May I offur my idee ta yu, Lootenant. I know whut yur orders wure but thangs change at times. Why don't yu send Phipps with a kouple men ta find Tye and I'll hep ya fin them thar Apache with tha rest uf tha patrol."

Paddock stood up looked up at Buff who was still sitting in the saddle. He nodded his head. "Thanks, Buff." He turned toward the men and spoke to Sergeant Baker. "Get two men to go with Corporal Phipps. The rest will go with me and Buff."

"Yes, Sir," Baker answered, He turned to the men.

"Privates Bates and Curry, front and Center." The two men stepped quickly forward. "You two will accompany Mr. Phipps and find Tye."

"Yo," Both men answered in unison. They mounted their horses and headed south with Phipps. The patrol headed east with Buff leading them, following the Apache tracks.

~~~

The Apache sitting straddle of Yancey reached down and grabbed a handful of hair and was touching his blade to Yancey's forehead. He was going to scalp him while he was alive. Tye fired the Henry, the bullet striking the brave square in the chest and exploding out his back. The impact of bullet hitting flesh propelled the Apache backwards, off Yancey. Before the repot of the rifle had died Tye fired a second shot at the closest Apache that was holding one of Yancey's arms. Tye was shocked at how quick the two reacted. His second shot only burned the brave on the shoulder when he moved to get away. His third shot splintered a branch on a mesquite and then silence…nothing moving. Not even a bird chirped as Tye frantically searched for a sign of one, or both Apaches.

He knew how an Apache thought and knew he had to move. They would be working their way, one to his left and the other to his right, to get him in crossfire. He moved to his right, backing down the slope and watching both right and left. He worked his way deeper into the brush. He stopped for a moment to listen. Hearing nothing; he moved a little more to the right, watching for any movement...listening for any sound. Sweat trickled down his neck even though it was fairly cool.

His senses were working overtime and he sensed the Apache behind him before he heard him. Tye rolled to his right and swung the Henry like a club as he rolled. The Apache was in mid-air, intending to jump on Tye's back, and drive his Bowie into the white man. The barrel of Tye's rifle struck the brave hard across the left shoulder. The force of the blow knocking him away from Tye; he hit the ground and rolled immediately to his feet, the Bowie still in his hand.

Tye, also jumping up, pulled his Bowie from his boot and squared off in front of the Apache. The Apache yelled something to the other brave. Tye spoke the language well enough to make out he was telling his companion to get over here. He knew he had to finish this quick or he was in trouble when the other one showed up. He could hear the other Apache coming through the brush. The Apache in front of him, like most Apaches, was no pilgrim to knife fighting. He held the blade low to the ground in his right hand and moved on the balls of his feet, his left arm out for balance and to ward off blows. A knife fight between two experienced fighters seldom left either man uncut.

The fighters faced each other, both moving to their right, feinting blows to see how the other reacted. Tye could pull his Colt from the holster and end it but he wasn't going to do that. The Apache could probably have shot him in the back earlier, but didn't. This was the warrior way, face to face with knives or tomahawks. A rifle shot startled both men. The second Apache stepped thru the brush, staggered a couple of steps and fell dead at the feet of the one facing Tye.

"WE'RE EVEN WATKINS...NEXT TIME I SEE YOU...YOU'RE DEAD," screamed Yancey. The sound of hooves striking rocks as he rode off reached Tye. The Apache came in low with a vicious swipe at Tye's stomach. Tye, cursing the fact Yancey was getting away, was almost caught flat-footed by the Apache and the blade missed his belly by one half inch as he took a quick step back, sucking in his stomach.

'This is one quick Apache,' Tye thought. 'You had better keep your mind on this, not something else or it might not end so good.' Tye feinted with his knife hand and when the Apache stepped back to avoid it, Tye stepped in with a vicious left hook that caught the warrior high on the right cheek. The Indian staggered backwards but didn't go down. A nasty cut was on his cheek with blood running down his neck and across his chest.

The blood seemed to enrage the Apache and he came in swinging his knife wildly. Tye was back pedaling when his foot hit a root and he fell backwards, hitting the ground hard. The Apache was in mid-air, coming down on him even before his back hit the ground. Tye's cat-like reaction saved him as he was rolling to his right the instant he hit the ground. The knife that was intended for Tye's chest, stuck harmlessly in the ground.

The Indian was up quickly and Tye, lying on his back kicked viciously at the knee of his adversary. A shriek of pain came from the Apache's mouth and he collapsed, holding his leg. Tye was on him instantly and drove the knife deep into the man's chest. A gasp was followed by a gurgling sound as blood came from his mouth. Tye rolled off him, gasping for breath as the Apache died.

~~~

Yancey was moving fast, intending to put as much distance as he could between himself and Watkins. He appreciated Tye's saving him from a lot of pain and a slow death. He paid Tye back some by killing one of the Apaches and could have killed the other but then, by doing so would have freed Watkins to chase him. He figured a good knife fight would give him a few minutes head start and who knows, the Apache could kill Tye. "Must be getting senile in my old age for letting him live; I could have shot all three if I had wanted to," he muttered out loud. It was the first decent thing he had done in a long time and it gave him a strange feeling...a good feeling, but it did not last long. "The bastard reminds me of a damn bloodhound the way he follows tracks and of a bulldog that won't let go of anything once he sets his mind to it." He reined his mount to a halt, and looked back over his shoulder. "I owed him though... and now we're even."

Kicking his mount back into an easy gallop, he had no idea where he was or where he was headed other than he was going south. The only two things he was sure of was his chest burned like hell where the skin had been ripped off and his belly needed some food.

He had covered several miles since the incident with Tye and the Apaches and saw nothing but sage, cactus and mesquite. A minute later however, in the distance, he saw what appeared to be a line of oak trees. 'If those are oaks, there should be some water.' He altered the direction his horse was traveling and headed for them. Five minutes later he was letting his horse drink in the small creek. The water was clear and cool. He knew he was some where south of Fort Clark but had no idea the creek was Los Moras Creek that originated at the fort. If he had known, he could have followed it straight back to the fort and straight to Tye's home... and Rebecca.

~~~

Buff and the patrol had been on the trail of the dozen or so Apaches all afternoon. He could tell by the sign that they were closing the gap. Apparently the Apaches did not have a clue there were any soldiers within miles and they were moving at a leisurely pace.

Buff reined up suddenly as the sound of gunfire reached him. He turned his horse and motioned for the patrol to come. Arriving in a clatter of steel shoes striking rocks and saber's clanging, the patrol pulled alongside of him. He motioned for them to be quiet.

They all heard it, gunfire and a lot of it coming from over the hill in front of them.

"Thank them 'paches dun found a homestead, Lootenant," Buff said spitting a wad of tobacco on the ground.

"Form a skirmish line," Paddock ordered. They advanced up the hill at a trot, Buff and the lieutenant in the middle with five men equally space about ten feet apart on either side. Reaching the crest they could see the homestead below in the fading light.

"Bugler...sound advance," Paddock ordered. At the sound of the bugle, the patrol charged down the slope. The Apaches were surprised but quickly turned their attention to the charging bluecoats. Half of the braves had repeating Henry's and the rest had single shot Sharps. Nasay directed a murderous fire at the troopers. The soldier next to Buff cart wheeled backwards off his horse as did the one on the end of the line. The soldiers, firing their pistols from the back of running horses had not scored a single hit. Paddock saw this and raised his hand to signal a halt. He sat his horse down on his haunches and dismounted before his mount had come to a halt.

"BEHIND THE ROCKS," he ordered as the others dismounted and followed him. Sergeant Bates slid in beside Buff, his left arm bloodied from a hole in the shoulder.

"That was a pretty damn stupid thing to do," he said grimacing in pain. "Can't believe he gave the order to charge in like that on open ground."

"Mabee so," Buff said, "but he wus rite out in front uf everwun, leeding tha charge. He may be a little green, but he don't lack no guts." He looked over at the hole in Baker's shoulder. "Luks like yu are hit pretee hard, Sargent." They both ducked behind the rock as bullets whistled over head.

About fifty yards separated the two groups. Sporadic fire came from the homestead as dark settled in. About thirty minutes after full dark, Buff stood up and walked in the direction where they Apaches were.

"BUFF, what the hell are you doing?" Paddock hollered.

"Apaches are gone Lootenant."

"No one heard them leave."

"Trust me, Lootenant, tha'r gone."

"You sure?...How?...I heard no sound." Buff walked over to Paddock. "Gud lesson fur yu. Jus remember, yu will only see an heer an Injun when he wants yu to." He walked closer to the homestead.

"HELLO THE HOUSE."

The door opened and a man and maybe a ten year old boy came out. "You soldier boys come on in," the old man hollered back.

"Got sum wunded men," Buff said shaking the man's hand.

"Bring them in. My missus will tend them." Paddock and the rest walked up at that time and the man shook each man's hand, thanking them. "Lieutenant, you bring them boys right on in," nodding toward Baker and another man that had been wounded. He saw the two bodies that lay across their saddles. "Sure am sorry about your men, Lieutenant."

"Thank you...they were good men; everyone here okay?"

"My oldest boy has a hole in his leg but other than being scared half to death, we're fine. Been dead for sure if you boys hadn't showed up when you did."

"You can thank that old mountain man over there, Shakespeare McDovitt. He kept us on the trail."

"That's Shakespeare McDovitt?" the man asked in an excited voice, "the mountain man?"

"Yes, sir, that's him."

"Friends call him, Buff?" the man questioned.

"Yes. That's his nickname," Paddock replied.

"I be damned," the man said as he turned to his young son. "Billy, go get them novels I read to you." He turned back to the lieutenant and stuck out his hand again. "Plum forgot my manners, Lieutenant, in all this excitement. My name's Bradley...Bill Bradley and that's my wife, Millie, over there. My older son is Jesse and you already met Billy."

"Proud to meet you, Mr. Bradley and certainly glad everyone is okay." Billy came back with the dime novels and Bill thumbed through them till he found the one he was looking for. "Look here, Lieutenant," he said handing the worn paperback to him.

"Hey Buff. Come over here a second." He handed the paperback to Buff. Buff looked at the cover that had a bearded man in buckskins that looked to be over six feet tall and very muscular looking. Buff stared at the cover for a moment.

"Well?" Paddock questioned.

Buff looked up, a tear rolling down his cheek, surprising the Lieutenant.

"What's the matter, Buff?" Buff sat down, starring at the artist version of the man who was his best friend.

"That's my frend, Ben...Ben Watkins, Tye's pa."

"But it has your name under the picture."

"Nev'r leern ta reed but my eyes or gud. That's Ben and a damn gud likness uf him."

"That's Tye's father?" Paddock questioned as other soldiers came over to look.

"Shur as thar's a God above." Buff answered, handing the picture to the soldiers. "Tha thar's Ben shur as I'm sitting heer."

"Looks a lot like Tye," one of the men said.

131

"When I ferst saw Tye, I tho't I wus luking at a ghost. He luks jus like Ben," Buff said. "Best damn fren I ev'r had."

There's a story in there about you, Watkins and Jim Bridger fighting off some Blackfoot on a small island in a river. Said there was almost a hundred of them red devils."

"Ya'll fought off a hundred Blackfoot?" an astonished trooper asked. Buff laughed harder than he had in a long time. When he stopped laughing he told the men.

"Tha thar's the truble with them thar story's you reed. We wure on a island okay but it wus a creek, not a riv'r and thar wus mabee a dozen or so Blackfut. Tha wus tha day me an Bridger leerned whut a wildcat we had fur a partner. Thos Blackfut came charg'n across tha creek a screeming and holloring like sumthang frum hell. We tuk several down with our long rifles and our old flintlock pistols. We didn't hav time ta reload so yung Ben jumped up yelling and screeming like them Blackfut. He wus swinging a tomeehawk in wun hand and his Bowie in tha uther. Saw him take down two then we sorta got buzee our ownselves. When them devils run off, old Ben wus still screemin and waving tha thar tomeehawk at them. Three lay deader than a peece of wood at his feet." He laughed again. "Yes Sir. We had us a reel wildcat fur a partner. But enuff of old storees. What's yur next step, Lootenant?"

"Get the dead and wounded back to Clark and continue pursuing the hostiles." Paddock answered with no hesitation."

"When?" Buff asked.

"As soon as it is light enough to follow tracks;" Buff turned to Mr. Bradley.

"Is thar anuther homestead east of heer?"

"There's the Wallace place about eleven miles southeast of here and the Milton's about six miles due east."

"I feel tha Apaches kno whar every homestead is, Lootenant. I bet tha hit tha Milton's about daylite. If Mr. Bradley heer can give me sum diretshuns, we mite jus be able to trap these heer Injuns.

"I can do better than that. I will take you. Least we can do for what you did for us. I sure don't want anything to happen to our friends, the Miltons. I'll get my horse. You can leave your dead and wounded here."

"Gud man thar, Lootenant?" Buff commented as Bradly walked off. They mounted their horses and waited for Bradley.

Gary McMillan

Chapter Sixteen

Tye made a cold camp in a clump of five foot cedars on the crest of a hill just before the sun dropped behind the hills to the west. There were a few scattered clouds on the horizon. Sunset was Tye's favorite time of the day. He loved a pretty one and he figured this was going to be one of those special ones because of the clouds. They looked darker and more menacing than they actually were because of the sun behind them. The edges of the clouds were trimmed in bright orange and the rays made streaks in the sky that ranged from a yellow to pinkish, to a blood red. "Damn pretty isn't it Sandy?" Sandy nickered and stomped one of his front hooves. Tye smiled and sat down on a rock and realized for the first time, he hadn't eaten since early this morning. He walked over to his saddlebags and took out some jerky. He broke off a good size chunk and chewed. Jerky didn't have much of a taste unless you were as hungry as Tye was...then it was steak. It was full dark by the time he finished the strip of jerky. He lay down on his bedroll, using his saddle as a pillow.

He wasn't sleepy but he was tired and stretching out felt good, even on the rocky ground. The stars were out with no moon to hinder their presence and they sparkled like diamonds. When he was young, Ben, his father, and him spent more nights sleeping under the stars than in their beds. His pa taught him to recognize most of the constellations and how paying attention to them and their location at certain times of the year might just help him someday if he was lost. He could also tell the time by them...not to the exact minute but close enough. He told Tye that ship captains had used them for hundreds of years to make their way across large bodies of water, even crossing the oceans.

He had worshipped his pa. Everything he was now, he owed to him. Ben spent hundreds of hours teaching Tye everything he needed to know to survive: tracking, hunting, shooting, knife fighting, and bare knuckle fighting and a thousand other things he would need to know. The one thing that always stood out was his preaching of being a man. This meant always keeping his word and being loyal to his friends. He preached about never backing down from a fight. He always told Tye that a man didn't have to win, but just never back down. He was a believer in always doing what you think is right. Tye could remember the day Ben died in his arms with an Apache bullet in his chest. With his last breath, he told Tye how much he loved him and his mother, Lori; he told Tye to take care of her.

While his father taught him what he needed to know to survive, Lori taught him how to read, write, and do numbers. He had never spent a day in a schoolroom but a person would never know it. His mother died two years after Ben died. Tye always thought she died of a broken heart. She was never the same after her Ben died. A lump formed in Tye's throat as he thought of Ben and her…he still missed them and always would.

He thought of Rebecca and wished he was lying beside her. Until they had gotten married a few months ago, he had always enjoyed sleeping under the stars more so than in bed. They were very happy and hoped to start a family before long. Tye wanted a boy that he could teach all he knew just as Ben had taught him. Of course though, he wouldn't complain if it was a girl. Main thing would be that everyone was healthy. He was thankful that Buff, Sergeant O'Malley, and Major Thurston were taking care of her with this animal he was chasing on the loose. He finally drifted off to sleep thinking of all these things.

~~~~

Darkness had engulfed Fort Clark. A light here and there from lamps could be seen. Headquarters was still open, at least Thurston's office was. He was sitting in his chair smoking his ever present cigar, trying to figure out what he needed to do…if anything. He had no idea what the situation was with Paddock's patrol. One of Tye's scouts come in earlier telling the major that a friend of his had spotted a fairly large band of Apaches coming from Mexico the day before. Thurston had dispatched the scout to see where they were going.

Most of the time, he loved his position as Post Commander. At times like this, he wasn't sure. He made a point of knowing everything that went on at the fort...even in Brackett. He had no control over what went on elsewhere and he hated it. Nothing was more stressful than sitting here wondering where his men were, if they were okay, and what the hell was going on with them.

Earlier, he had been the guest of First Sergeant O'Malley and his wife for dinner. He had enjoyed his visit with them, Rebecca, and the Turley children. The children had been taken in by the O'Malley after their parents were killed a few months ago by the Apache. Their grandparents were also killed in the raid. The Turleys had been very close friends of Tye and he had sworn over their graves to get the children back from the Apaches. In a daring rescue by himself, he had freed them and some other children from the Apache camp, killing the Apache leader, Tanza, in a fierce hand to hand fight.

Thurston's job of protecting the settlers was a tough one, but it was one he cherished. He loved this land and had a great respect for the brave and hardy people trying to settle here and make a life for themselves. He intended to make it a safe place. It was a tough job for a man with limited manpower. He was trying to protect people over an area that ran forty miles north and south and thirty miles east and west of Fort Clark a vast area for one fort to protect. He was grateful for having a man like Tye to help him. He was also fortunate to have a staff of good, capable officers that could be depended on.

He finished his cigar, blew out the lamp, and walked outside. He took a deep breath of the fresh, nippy, fall air and sat down on the porch. The fresh air smelled good and it cleared his head some. He took out another cigar but decided not to light it. He stuck it in his mouth, stood up and walked to his quarters enjoying the cool air.

137

~~~

Yancey had made camp just at full dark. He decided to rest for a couple hours then head east for a mile or so then swing back north, toward Clark. Hell, his chest burned so much he couldn't sleep if he had too. He had been without a woman long enough and that need had over shadowed his good sense. He had pictured Rebecca in his mind many times. Tye was a good looking man so he figured she had to be a looker. He would find her, take his time and enjoy himself before killing her. Her death would enrage Tye to the point he would get careless and he would take advantage of that.

It was full dark when he rode out. He gave the horse a free rein as the horse could see a lot better than he could in the dark. He knew it was risky traveling on this terrain at night with no moon but he knew he could put several miles between him and the scout by daylight. He could rest some then and watch his back trail at the same time.

Chapter Seventeen

The patrol pulled to a halt about a mile from the Milton homestead. They had not stopped since leaving the Bradley place and the men and horses were exhausted. It was now a few minutes past midnight and the men had been on the move since before daylight yesterday. The order was given to take care of the horses and then get some rest. It would be a cold camp with no unnecessary noise. The horses were fed, watered, and tied to a picket line. Sentry schedule was set and the men turned in after eating a few bites of jerky and a dry biscuit washed down with warm water from their canteens.

"Do you think the Apaches are here, Buff?" Paddock whispered as Buff sat down on his bedroll beside him.

"Tha are heer, Lootenant." Buff whispered back. "Be willing ta bet we are kamped within a mile or so uf 'um."

"Your thinking that doesn't make me feel very comfortable," Paddock expressed.

Buff chuckled and lay down. "When thangs get quiet and everyone's asleep I will slip out uf kamp and find 'em."

"By yourself?" Paddock whispered. "That's out of the question."

"Do yu or anee uf yur men have these?" Buff asked holding up his foot with the moccasin boots.

"No; but what does that have to do with anything?"

"Listen," Buff said. "Yu can heer yur sentries walking frum heer. Tha thar is whut I'm talking abut. No way yu or yur men with them boots on kud sneek up on even a deff Injun an we ain't chasin deff Injuns but yung bucks tha kud heer a pin drop."

"I guess I understand that, Buff, but I..." he was cut off by Buff.

"We hav ta know whar tha are Lootenant. Tha's tha botum line uf tha situashun."

"Don't guess we have much of a choice if you put it that way."

"It's settled then. Let's git ta sleep." Buff replied.

Two hours later, Buff was out of camp unnoticed by the sentries. He thought it was funny. 'Damn Apache would have no trouble sneaking into camp if an old man like me can get out.' He shook his head. He moved silently, working his way carefully around the cactus and mesquite. He smelled the smoke of the campfire before he found it. He spotted one Apache that was with the horses and no other anywhere. Apaches were like a lot of other tribes, they depended on their horse herd to let them know of anyone near. They seldom had more than one sentry.

Having located them he headed back to camp sneaking again past the guards. He didn't want to get them in trouble so he walked back and got one of 'em's attention. The guard stiffened at the sound then relaxed. "OH, it's you, Buff."

"It's me sunny. Listen heer, I snuk out of this kamp about an hour ago and jus now snuk bac in. Yu bett'r leern ta be a little more alert out heer or yu gonna git yurself and a lot uf yur frends kilt."

"You left and came back?" the guard asked, astonished that he did not know.

"Yep. Left and found tha Apache kamp. Yu tell yur frends over thar ta sta alert or thar scalp's gonna be hangin on an Apache lance."

The young guard swallowed the lump in his throat. "Ye...Yes Sir. I...I will."

Buff walked over to where Lieutenant Paddock was. He found him awake, sitting on his bedroll pulling on his boots. He looked up at Buff.

"Did you find the Apache camp?" he asked anxiously.

"Yep. Bout a mile frum heer. Thar's tweve or maybe thirteen uf them. Tha don't have anee idée we are nearby."

"Why do you say that?"

"No sentrees. Onlee got wun man watchin tha hosses."

"Do you have a plan?"

"Yes, sir, I do. I wuld like ta heer yours ferst tho, Lootenant." Paddock finished pulling his boots on, stood up and placed his hat on his head. He hesitated answering for a minute. He stared at the ground, thinking. Finally, just as Buff was gonna ask him again, he spoke.

"The best plan would be to surround the camp well before daylight and surprise them at daybreak."

"Wal I be damned. Yu mite jus make a gud officer yet." Buf said laughing... "Tha thar wud be tha thing ta do. Simple, but I didn't kno fur shor if'n yu had kommon sense ar not. Figgered yu wud jus say lets charge into them like we did yesterday." He laughed again and slapped Paddock on the shoulder. Paddock wasn't sure if he just got a compliment or not.

The camp slowly came alive with men standing up, scratching and stretching. It was earlier than normal so there was some grumbling among the troops. They were surprised when they were told today they would be infantry instead of cavalry. The plan was outlined to them so each man knew what to do. They moved out of camp following Buff with the order of being absolute quite, no talking whatsoever. There were no sabers, canteens, or anything else that might make any unnecessary noise. Their Sharps rifles were left in their boots on their saddles. Each man carried his revolver and nothing else. Three of the greenest troops were left in camp to watch the horses.

Silently, the men moved through the cactus and brush for twenty minutes before Buff signaled a halt. He turned to Paddock and whispered, "Tha kamp is jus over that rise thar," he said pointing. "We need ta split into two grups. Sum uf yur men can go with me and tha rest with yu."

"Mr. Bradley, you will stay here." Paddock ordered.

"But I nee..." he tried to reply but was cut off by Buff.

"Tha lootenants right. Yu have a nice famlee. I kudn't live with myself if something happed ta yu when it wusn't nessarry. Yu jus sta heer."

They circled the camp of the sleeping Indians, staying hidden behind the sage and mesquites. The order had been given not to shoot until Buff signaled for them too. Buff checked the stars and figured they had about an hour before first light. It was too dark now for accurate shooting. He made himself comfortable, and waited. A minute later an Apache got up and walked to the edge of camp to relieve himself and spotted one of the soldiers. Buff threw his Bowie striking the Apache in the back just as he shouted the alarm. The camp came alive instantly with Apaches as they jumped from the blankets and grabbing their weapons.

"FIRE," Buff shouted and instantly the early morning quietness was shattered by the roar of guns, Apache war cries, and screams of wounded and dying men. The Apaches quickly rallied around Nasay and on his order, all charged the line of troopers that were between them and their pony herd…Paddock's side. The men directly in their path never stood a chance as they were quickly over run by the sheer number of the devils, knives and tomahawks slicing into them. Most of the shots fired in the morning darkness missed their marks. At least seven Apaches made their way with Nasay to the pony herd and fled.

There was nothing the soldiers could do except listen to the fading sound of running horses. Their mounts were a mile or so away. Paddock grabbed a private and told him to get a casualty report and the number of dead hostiles. Paddock walked over to where the Apaches had over run their line of defense and looked at three dead troopers and a fourth that was badly wounded. He sat down feeling pretty low. He now has had seven or eight dead men under his command in less than twenty-four hours. Buff saw this and walked over and sat down, placing his hand on the Lieutenant's shoulder. The private came back and gave his report. "Three dead and three wounded, one serious. Five Apaches are dead and don't know how many are wounded but I am sure some are." Paddock just nodded.

"Bad luck, Lootenant. Jus plain bad luck. That thar buck jus tuk a bad time ta take a leek. Twern't no fault uf yurs."

"How many got away?" Paddock asked not looking up.

"My guess abut seven or eight," the old mountain man answered.

"Sergeant."

"Yes sir," the sergeant answered.

"Gather the dead and wounded and we will head back to camp to get the horses.

"Right away Sir."

~~~

Daylight found Tye where Yancey had stopped at dark last night and rested. He scouted around and found the tracks headed east. He toed the stirrup and swung into the saddle, kicked Sandy into a trot and followed Yancey east. He knew he was several hours behind since Yancey had been traveling most of the night. He could tell by the tracks Yancey's horse was walking, being real careful in the dark and this might just help him close the gap. Tye was trotting Sandy when he reined him in sharply.

"Damn you Yancey," he cursed. The tracks suddenly veered north. "Damn you." He looked north where Yancey was headed. 'He's going to try it. He's going for Rebecca,' he thought to himself. He reached down and patted Sandy on the neck.

"I'm gonna need you big boy. We've got to catch the bastard before he hurts Rebecca," he said out loud. Sandy snorted and stomped his hooves as if to say 'let's go.' Tye put his heels in Sandy's flanks and held on as the horse was at a full gallop in three strides. Yancey's tracks were easy to see, even at a gallop.

After thirty minutes, Tye pulled Sandy down to a walk, then a halt. He dismounted to study the tracks. He was surprised he was no more than two hours behind. He was pleased and followed the tracks on foot, leading Sandy so he could recuperate and be ready for the final push.

After twenty minutes of walking he remounted Sandy and was again at a full gallop. A minute later he again reined him to a halt. He jumped down and studied the ground. There was a hell of lot of tracks, some were unshod.

"Apaches," he exclaimed. He could tell by looking closer that the shod tracks were over the unshod ones. He could tell they were cavalry tracks by the shoe prints. He just didn't know if they were down from Clark or from Fort Inge. His choice was plain to him. 'Let the soldiers take care of the Apache, I've got to catch me a killer.' He remounted and once again was on Yancey's trail.

~~~

Yancey was taking a breather. He was tired and his horse was worn out. He had come across the little creek he had seen yesterday, or at least he figured it was the same. He took some of the cool water and splashed it on his chest. It burned for a second then felt good. The wound was festering and turning red. He figured he was going to be in trouble in a few hours. A sudden thought came to him and he looked at the creek and the direction it came from. "Los Moras," he muttered to himself. "I bet this is Los Moras Creek."

If he followed it, it would lead him to the fort...and Tye's home. He had heard his home was on the creek just on the edge of the fort. He felt a sudden surge of energy and stood up to walk to his horse. He happened to look over his shoulder and froze. A quarter mile behind him was Tye. His horse was at a gallop and the gap between them was closing fast. He looked frantically for a place he could ambush the scout. He glanced where his horse was and didn't think Tye could see him till it was too late.

He spied a large stump of an oak on the bank of the creek. The trunk of the tree which had fell no telling how many years ago; lay at a ninety degree angle to the creek on the bank above where Yancey was. He scrambled up the bank and staying low, jumped behind the trunk. He took off his hat and peered over the trunk to see where that damn Watkins was. "Shit," he uttered. He could not see him. 'Where in hell could he have gone?' he wondered. His head pivoted in all directions, scanning the terrain everywhere in front of him. His gaze settled on a stand of seven or eight foot cedars about one hundred yards away. He detected a little movement...or did he. His eyes strained to see through the maze of branches that were covered in the green, prickly like leaves.

"There you are," he mumbled. "Gotcha you sonofabitch." He could make out Sandy thru the cedars. He figured Tye was in there too. He had time to wait. He would wait till the scout showed himself and then it would be all over. He smiled...waited, licking his lips in anticipation.

~~~

Tye knew from the tracks he was close to Yancey. That extra sense told him he had better be damn careful. He led Sandy into the stand of cedars and hobbled him there. He gave him a drink from his hat and then took a good drink himself from the canteen. Tye, lying on his stomach so he could not be outlined by Yancey looking in the cedars, studied the area ahead of him. Yancey had been following the creek for awhile so he figured he would still be. However, he could see a long ways and saw no rider. 'The bastard is holed up, waiting for me to show myself,' he thought to himself. This made a dangerous situation even worse unless he could spot him.

He remembered what his pa told him one time years ago. When tracking a man and you lose him, put yourself in his place and see what you would do. Tye had done this in the past and it proved to be right most of the time. He looked for places where a man could hide. After five minutes of studying the lay of the land, he figured the only place to be was behind that huge old oak trunk that lay by the creek. 'That's where I'd be,' he thought.

The only problem with this idea, or thinking, was that if you guessed wrong you could be blindsided from somewhere else. He studied on it some more after checking the sun. 'Got plenty of daylight left' he mused. He waited. If he was right and Yancey was behind the oak he had a great defensive position and if I was moving, I'd be an easy target.

He thought of different plans but it all came down to a simple solution. He had to know for sure where Yancey was and the only way to find out was to give him a target to shoot at. He thought back a few months earlier when he was in a similar situation. He was pinned down in a ditch alongside The Old Mail Road and he exposed himself to draw fire where he could see where his attackers were. It worked but you have to have a little luck and pray they miss. He saw a large boulder to his right about thirty yards away. Beyond the boulder was a deadfall that was another twenty or so yards farther to the right. He could not see beyond the deadfall but if there was another place to hide, he might just be able to flank Yancey. He gathered himself for the first part, getting to the boulder. Taking a deep breath, he jumped up and ran in a zigzag pattern toward the boulder, expecting a bullet every step.

~~~

Buff was on the remaining Apaches' trail less than an hour after the dawn attack. The Apaches had headed south but shortly swung west, toward Mexico which was about thirty or so miles away. 'Tha are running thos damn hosses to hard,' Buff thought. He held his mount to an easy gait. The tracks were plain enough and no trouble following even from the back of a horse being held to a slow gallop.

This time, the patrol was right behind him, maybe fifty yards instead of the usual two or three hundred yards. He glanced over his shoulder and saw the company's banner flapping in the wind above the dust and the men, who even at a gallop were staying two abreast. The sight always made him feel good. In fact, he was enjoying this chase, feeling the wind in his face and the sun on his back. 'Makes me feel alive,' he thought.

He suddenly reined in and jumped off his mount. He looked at the tracks and smiled. Paddock and the patrol arrived in a cloud of dust.

"What do we have, Buff?" Paddock asked.

Buff, never turned to look at the lieutenant, instead was studying the terrain ahead. "We are going to find them pretty quick, Sir."

"How do you figure that?"

"Luk at th traks. Tha stride is getting shorter, signs uf tiring hosses. Thay are going ta be afoot before long."

"That's no problem for an Apache, Buff." Phipps said. "Tye says an Apache on foot, in a long race, can run down a horse."

"Most Injuns I kno can run. This heere won't be a long race. We ar staing abut an hour behind them. If we kan keep our mounts fairly fresh, we kan catchum when thay git on foot. We need ta walk our mounts fur abut thirty minutes or so then git bac on their trail hard and fast... We have pleenty uf daylite left."

Chapter Eighteen

The bullet whistled by Tye's head before he heard the report of the rifle. A mesquite branch split as he heard the report of the second shot. Reaching the boulder he slid in behind it and rock fragments stung his hand as a third bullet struck the boulder. 'Guess I guessed right as to where he was,' Tye thought as he wiped his bloody hand on the grass. There were two cuts on the back of his left hand, painful, but not serious. He took off his kerchief and wrapped his hand.

Tye knew he had to get to the deadfall if he was going to have a chance to flank Yancey. He grabbed a quick look. It was twenty yards to the deadfall and only a couple of small shrubs between where he was and where he was going. He checked the Henry and was thankful for the second time that he had it instead if his single shot Sharps. He could put down enough fire to maybe keep Yancey's head down long enough for him to move to the deadfall. He waited a few seconds to catch his breath and raised up and fired as fast as he could work the lever and chamber new shells. He sprinted toward the deadfall, firing as he ran. He could see chips from the fallen oak Yancey was behind. He saw Yancey raise up and take aim. He saw the smoke from the barrel of the rifle and the stock on his Henry splintered in his hand as Yancey's bullet shattered it. "Dammit," Tye hollered, cursing as he fell behind the deadfall. He looked at the now useless Henry and threw it away.

For the first time, Tye felt a foreboding, a feeling that he might fail for the first time in his life. He thought of Rebecca and what this sorry bastard might do to her. He thought of Buff and the possibility of him being hurt or killed...all because he failed to kill

Yancey. "YANCEY," he said, spitting the name out in disgust; "You sorry piece of horse shit." Suddenly he thought of his pa and one of the things he had always preached. "A man can never think straight or do his best when he is wrought-up. He has to relax to think straight," he used to say. 'That's what I need to do,' Tye thought to himself. He took his Colt out of its holster and checked the loads. Placing it back in his holster, he sat back and relaxed. He wanted to gather his thoughts before taking his next step, whatever that was going to be.

~~~

Lieutenant Paddock had given the order to remount and the patrol was moving at a trot, following Buff. Buff told Paddock while they were walking their mounts that when the Apaches' horses gave out and the warriors were a foot, we had best be careful. They would be like a cornered animal...more dangerous than ever.

Twenty minutes later they came upon the first two horses. They had floundered and the riders cut their throats. The two braves were now running and Buff could see their footprints mixed in with the horses. For the next thirty minutes, a horse or two was found every half mile or so; Buff reined in, deciding to wait on the patrol after he figured they found the last of the horses.

Paddock reined his mount in beside Buff.

"Gonna git touchy frum heer on, Lootenant. Tha men bettur be reddy fur aneethang. Theese heer 'Patches are gonna fite wunce tha see tha can't outrun us. Figger tha will drop wun or two bac to try and slow us down sum. These will not be yung warriors tha sta behin but old, seasoned ones, and tha will be meener than aneethang yu ever did see. Seen Injuns when tha git themselves worked up take three or fore bullets ta stop. We may end it tuday, but it's gonna git damn bloodee." He spoke to Phipps who was sitting on his horse on the other side of Paddock.

"Korporal, yu sta behind me a few yards and watch this ole geezers' bac. Shoot ferst and ask questions later...okay?"

Phipps looked at Paddock for approval. Paddock nodded his okay. "I'll be behind you, Buff," Phipps promised. Buff nodded and rode ahead. Phipps fell in behind him about twenty yards and Paddock and the patrol about the same distance behind Phipps. The men had their Sharps out, cocked and pointed to the sky, the rifle butts resting on their thighs. Tension was high as each had heard what Buff said. From what they had seen the last two days, they had no doubt that the old mountain men knew what he was talking about. It was fixing to get bloody.

~~~

Tye looked quickly for his next spot to run to. "Damn," he cursed again. There was no cover for at least twenty yards. He sat back down to think what his next move would be. He was in a pickle but then, so was Yancey. Neither could move without chancing getting shot. Yancey could move down the creek, staying below the level of the ground but his back would be exposed to Tye for at least twenty yards.

They were only about thirty yards apart now and Yancey figured Tye was a damn good shot with his sidearm. He figured by running he would get hit, maybe not a killing hit, but one that might disable him. That would lead to his capture and hanging. That was not going to happen. He would die before he spent another minute in a stinking Yankee prison and any death was better than getting one's neck stretched. He looked at the sun and figured there was at least two hours of daylight. It was going to be a long two hours he figured, or maybe an eternity for one of them. He was thankful for the rocky ground. It would be impossible for either of them to move about without making some kind of noise. He sat there with complete silence all around him...no birds chirping, no ground squirrels running about...nothing, not even the ever present buzzards that one could always see floating through the air. The only sound he could hear was his own heart pounding, and it seemed loud enough for that damn scout to hear it beating.

Tye had thought of a dozen plans but had found fault with each, and discarded each quickly. One more thing his pa had taught him was that when all else fails, tackle the problem head on. "I wonder if he was thinking about a situation like this though," Tye mumbled to himself. Despite the situation, he smiled at the thought. 'Maybe that might just work,' he thought. 'With these moccasins, Yancey might not hear me till it's too late. It might just be the best thing to do. If this doesn't end before dark, he might get away.'

He raised himself up on one knee and took off his hat. He looked at the sky, and then bowed his head. *"Lord, I hope you are listening. I know the only time you seem to hear from me is when I need something. But Lord, this is not so much for me but for two people I care about. If it's your will that I live through this so be it but if you don't, please protect Rebecca and my friend Buff. Please protect them. I ask all this in your name, Lord. Amen."*

He stood up slowly, and looked over the boulder toward where Yancey was. He saw nothing. He looked in all directions, making sure the man somehow had not moved to another spot. Seeing nothing, he stood up, and taking a deep breath, began taking one careful step after another. He moved silently toward the oak where Yancey was, placing each foot down carefully. His heart was pounding and sweat ran down his forehead, stinging his eyes. With his left arm, he wiped the sweat away with his sleeve. He was half way there, maybe ten yards away. Three or four quick strides and he would be there. But then again Yancey could raise and fire at the sound and might just get lucky and hit him. 'Sound... a sound might just trick him into exposing himself,' he thought. Looking around, he found a small limb close to his feet. Bending down, he picked it up, never taking his eyes off where Yancey was. He threw the stick to Yancey's left. It was a high arching throw and before it hit, Tye had his Colt cocked, aimed where he figured Yancey to be...or would be.

~~~

Buff reined his mount to a halt. Ahead, where the Apache tracks led, was a jumble of huge boulders, shrubs, and every other conceivable thing that could hide an Injun. If there was ever a perfect spot for an ambush, this was it. He took his chew out of his shirt pocket, and bit off a piece. He chewed furiously for a few seconds, then spit a wad at an unseen object on the ground. Placing the remaining chew back in his pocket, he waited on the patrol.

It only took a minute for them to arrive. Phipps looked at what lay ahead.

"My God, Buff. We ain't going through that are we?"

"Tha's tha Lootenant's kall." Buff answered.

"What's the lieutenant's call?" Paddock asked, riding up to them.

Buff nodded toward the huge boulders. "Tha 'Paches went in thar. Got me self a feelin tha gitting them out ain't gonna be ezee if'n tha or still in thar."

Paddock looked at the jumble of house sized boulders with cactus, shrubs, and cedar growing out of almost ever crevice in them. He took off his hat and kerchief. He wiped his face and neck, retied the kerchief, and placed the hat back on his head. He knew this was fixing to be his biggest decision in his young career. He was sure that somewhere along the line at the Point, they discussed what to do in a situation like this. Then again, not too many things they studied did concern fighting Apaches who didn't exactly follow rules. He figured times like this was what Thurston was talking about when he said all his learning wasn't worth a damn out here. He needed help on this one.

"What do you think, Buff?"

Buff spit a wad of tobacco on the ground before answering.

"Seven or eight 'Paches went in thar. Let me ride around ta tha uther side ta see how manee kum out."

Paddock nodded. "Take Phipps with you. We'll stay here."

Buff nodded. "Don't," he said, "go in thar fur anee reason even if yu heer shuting frum us."

Paddock nodded his head. "Understood."

"Let's go, Phipps," Buff said. They headed to the left of the mess at a gallop.

Paddock studied the area. The boulders seem to just rise out of the earth at this spot. The rest of the terrain was mostly flat with a few rolling hills. He figured the boulders were spewed from the bowels of the earth thousands of years ago, probably during an earthquake. The boulders seem to cover an area maybe a hundred and fifty yards wide, and a quarter mile in length. He was new out here but they looked like a dangerous place to try and go through.

He was glad Buff was here to help make some of these decisions that his inexperience prevented him from knowing what to do. He came out here thinking he knew everything and here he was getting taught by a man who couldn't read or write. He had to chuckle to himself at that thought.

"Corporal Christian," Paddock hollered.

"Here, Sir."

"Have the men dismount. We will wait until we hear back from Buff and Phipps before moving out. We'll wait there," he said pointing to a stand of mesquite large enough to offer a little shade. "Make sure the men keep their weapons handy and assign one man to watch those rocks to make sure no one comes out." Paddock had heard how Christian had assisted in bringing in Yancey a few weeks ago. He had heard nothing but good things about him and Phipps. He looked for Christian to take Sergeant Baker's place since Baker was back at the Bradley's with a hole in his shoulder. He handed his reins to a private and sat down to wait.

At the far end of the rocks, Buff dismounted and walked back and forth while Phipps walked beside him, watching the rocks, his Sharps cocked in case the Apache made a break for it.

"Kan't find no traks, Phipps. Tha have run as fur as tha are going ta go. I tale ya wun thang, this here situashun is fixen ta git nasty."

They mounted up and rode along the opposite side of the rocks going back to Paddock, making sure no tracks were there.

Chapter Nineteen

Tye stood perfectly still, legs apart, his pistol in his right hand aimed just above the trunk of the oak. He stood on the bank of the creek waiting for the stick he had thrown to hit the ground, hoping Yancey would rise and fire at the sound. When he did, he would kill him. It seemed an eternity before the stick crashed into a mesquite, shaking the limbs. Yancey stood up and fired his Henry several times as fast as he could work the lever, spreading the shots all around the mesquite. Shattered mesquite limbs and prickly cactus were flying everywhere. He fired until his Henry clicked on an empty chamber.

Tye was slightly behind him and squeezed the trigger. He let off the pressure just before the hammer fell. He could not do it...he could not shoot a man in the back, even a man like Yancey. He just stood there, his pistol aimed square in the middle of Yancey's back...waiting.

Yancey stood still looking at the mesquite he had shredded. Suddenly he stiffened, sensing he had been tricked. He turned his head slowly around, looking at Tye.

"I hope you go for your pistol, Yancey" The outlaw was stubborn, mean, and cruel, whatever you wanted to say about him, he was. One thing he wasn't was stupid. He looked at Tye with cold, dead eyes, and his expression showing no fear. He dropped the rifle and turned slowly toward Tye.

"Take your left hand and real careful like, take the pistol out of its holster and throw it away." Yancey did as he was told and tossed the gun away but if looks could kill, Tye would be a dead man. "Step out from behind the tree," Tye instructed. Again, Yancey did as he was told. Tye could see the man was tense, ready to spring if there was any chance. Tye did not intend to give him that chance. When Yancey had done as he was told, Tye relaxed some and took a step. As he did, the bank he was standing on gave way. Tye fell backwards into the creek, hitting hard on his back. The jolt caused him to lose his grip on the pistol and it splashed somewhere in the creek.

He looked up and saw Yancey in mid-air, the blade of the Bowie flashing in the sunlight, coming down on him. He rolled to the side and the Bowie hit where his chest had been an instant earlier. Tye was instantly on his feet, his Bowie magically appearing in his hand. He had pulled the Bowie without thinking, a result of years of depending on his reflexes to keep him alive.

Yancey was up just as quick. He took a wild swing at Tye's mid-section, missing badly.

"You are no knife-fighter, Yancey...give up." Tye said calmly.

"I'm gonna gut you like I would a deer you damn Yankee bastard," he screamed. He attacked Tye with a fury that surprised Tye and Yancey's blade cut deep into Tye's left arm that he was holding in front of himself for balance.

The blood only made Yancey attack more furiously, wildly swinging his Bowie at Tye. Tye, over his surprise, let his instincts take over. The next swing Yancey took, Tye waited till the arm passed and was extended past him. He struck down with his Bowie and cut Yancey's knife hand so severely that all feeling left the arm and he dropped the knife. Tye backed up, surprising Yancey.

"Pick it up with your other hand, Yancey."

The man slowly bent down and picked it up with his left hand, never once taking his eyes off the scout. He immediately stabbed at Tye. Tye pared the knife with his knife and swung a vicious left at Yancey's chin. Knuckle met chin, and the outlaw was knocked backwards several feet on his back. He dropped his knife, lying there dazed. Tye, standing over him, reached down and grabbed the man's collar and lifted him to his feet. He held him there till Yancey regained his senses. He then turned him loose and backed up. Tye reached down and picked up the knife Yancey had dropped, handing it back to him.

Yancey looked into Tye's eyes and felt fear for the first time in his life. 'This crazy man wants me to fight...daring me to fight.' He threw his knife away and stood there...both men looking at each other with burning hate. When Tye realized the outlaw was not going to fight him he stooped and replaced the Bowie in his boot. He squared up in front of Yancey and stuck out his chin.

"Take your best shot, Yancey." Yancey did, his left catching Tye on the cheek and knocking him back a foot or so. Tye reached up and felt of his jaw. "If that's the best you got you bastard, you are in for a long day." Tye stepped into the man with a right to the belly, and when the bandit bent over holding his stomach, Tye's knee caught him flush on the nose, snapping his head back. A left caught Yancey just above his right ear and another right was buried just above his belt buckle. Tye grabbed him by the back of his collar as he doubled up and pulled him upright. He let him stand there; swaying from side to side and carefully measured him. He swung his right fist with all the hate, all the fury he could muster exploding at once. The blow caught Yancey just below the left eye, crushing the cheek bone. The outlaw hit the ground like a sack of potatoes and did not move. His eyelids fluttered a couple time and then closed. Tye straddled the man's chest and pressed the point of his knife against Yancey's throat. He tensed his muscles to make the push that would end everything. He could see the faces of his friends this sonofabitch had killed. He thought of what this animal was going to do to Rebecca. Now was the time to end it. It would be so easy to push the blade into his throat and nobody would know. He hesitated, and then stood up. He could not kill a man in cold blood...not even Yancey. "Damn," he cursed.

Tye sat down, breathing heavily. He took off his kerchief and wrapped his arm where Yancey's blade had sliced into it. He got up off the ground and took Yancey's bandana and tied it around the cut on the outlaw's wrist. He then took a long drink from the creek. He found Yancey's horse, and after cutting off three feet of rope, tied the unconscious mans hands together. With that done he sat down hard on his butt, legs crossed, 'Indian style.' He was suddenly completely overwhelmed by a feeling of relief that swept over him...as if the whole world was just lifted off his shoulders. He looked up at the blue sky. *"Thank You, Lord. Thank You,"* he said, a lump forming in his throat as he thought of Rebecca finally being safe. A tear ran down his cheek which he quickly wiped away. "Thank You," he said again lying back on the ground. He relaxed for the first time in what seemed a lot longer than three days.

~~~

Buff and Phipps arrived back to where Paddock waited. Both men dismounted and took a drink from their canteens as an impatient Paddock waited.

"Well?" Paddock said as Buff wiped the drops of water from his lips.

"We got us a situashun heer, Lootenant. Tha ain't runnin no more. Tha are in them thar rocks and tha are radee ta die. Kourse, tha intend ta take as manee uf us with them as tha kan."

Paddock turned and looked back at the rocks which were a little over a hundred yards away. He could feel eyes looking at him...waiting for him. He reached up and stuck a finger between his neck and kerchief and tried to loosen it some. Suddenly, it felt like it was choking him. A lump was in his throat and he was scared...not scared so much of dying but scared of making a decision that would get all his men killed. He turned back to Buff.

"Wh...what do think?"

"Kaution, Lootenant. Proceed with kaution. This heer is going ta be klose in, hand ta hand fiting. No place fur tenderfuts this time." He spit a wad of tobacco on the ground. My idée wud be ta spread out and work our way thru ta tha uther end. Have tha men pare up. Have wun in front rootin out tha Injuns and the uther behind him, protecting his bac. Nuthin but pistols. Don't thank thar will be room ta swing a rifle up an fire. We kan muve all at tha same time."

Paddock thought about this for a few seconds and then summoned his men around him. "I want each of you to pair up with another man. One will be in front of the other as we move through the rocks. The man in back will never and I mean never lose sight of your partner in front of you. You are to keep any Apaches off his back. Men, this is going to be tough. We will try to stay in an even line as we move through but don't get into a rush. No talking, no noise...understood." A chorus of Yo's and nodding heads indicated each man understood the situation.

"Absher..."Buff said, speaking in a low tone. "Yu kum with me." Private Absher hurried over and looked at Buff.

"Why did you pick me? I'm probably the greenest man here."

"Time ta be a soldier sonny. I figure yu ta be jus like yur grandpappy and I trusted him manee times."

"I'll keep them off your back for sure," Absher said.

"Never tho't anee different," Buff said patting the youngster on the shoulder.

Paddock was nervous. He stood straight, swallowed the bile that was trying to come up and turned toward where Buff and Absher stood. Buff took the middle of the rocks, Phipps was on his left with Christian following and Paddock was on his right, with Private Bates watching his back. To Phipp's left was Private Reynolds and Private Roberts watching his back

"Re...ready?" the nervous lieutenant asked. All the men nodded. "Move out."

The front man of each group moved out. All were in the rocks except one man who was left with the horses. Paddock had not thought about leaving the horses unguarded till Buff casually mentioned a cavalry man wasn't much good without his horse. He appreciated the comment because it would have been embarrassing if they lost them. He knew Buff could have said something in front of the men, but didn't. He appreciated that.

They were fifty feet into the rocks and found nothing so far...except a hell of lot of sweat and frayed nerves. Every man expected an Apache to appear any second, and any step could be their last. Suddenly an Apache appeared out of no where, almost like a ghost. He stepped out from his hiding place and with a vicious swipe, swung his war club at Buff's head. Buff, from years of fighting Indians was not caught off guard. His reflexes were still sharp and he ducked under the club and swung his pistol at the Apache at the same time, catching the man in the ribs. The blow did not crack any ribs on the Apache only because Buff's strength wasn't what it use to be. The brave recovered and charged back at Buff. A bullet struck the Indian in the side of the head and blood, brain matter, and skull fragments splattered on the wall of the boulder he had been hidden behind.

Buff turned and nodded to Absher...who nodded back, flashing a big smile at him. Buff turned back to the task ahead and moved forward. A scream to his left, on the other side of Phipps was followed by a rifle blast...then silence. All the men had stopped moving. Buff turned to Phipps and said.

"We won't go no further till yu check an see whut happened." Phipps moved to his left and found a dead Apache that was on top of a trooper lying on his back with a knife in his chest. "What happened?" Phipps asked Roberts, who had been watching Reynolds back.

"It was so sudden, Phipps. I didn't have a chance. He came from no where and stuck that knife in my friend's chest. It...It was so quick," he mumbled, dropping to his knees and placing his hand on his friend's head.

Phipps shook him on the shoulder and said. "We got to keep moving, Roberts. Let's go," he added picking up the man by the arm. "Let's go."

Phipps hollered at Paddock. "One man down, Sir; Private Reynolds; Roberts killed the Apache." He was quite for a few seconds while he moved back into position. Roberts moved closer to Phipps. Christian could see both men.

'Damn! Do they think I'm some kind of magician and I can watch both men's back,' he thought to himself, shaking his head.

Paddock said. "Roberts, watch their backs."

"Figures," Roberts mumbled under his breath. He replaced the one spent shell in the chamber, giving him six bullets again. "Ready, Sir," he said.

"Move forward," Paddock ordered. 'Two down, four or five to go,' he thought to himself.

~~~

Tye raised himself up and saw the sun was thirty minutes from setting. "Musta fell asleep," he said out loud. Quickly regaining his bearings, he took a quick glance at Yancey. He hadn't moved but wasn't dead. Tye could see his chest rising and falling. He slowly and unsteadily stood up. He seemed drained of all energy. His arm hurt like hell and his stomach hurt almost as much. He couldn't do much about his arm but could his stomach. He hadn't eaten since before daylight and that was just some jerky. He walked to the creek and kneeling, took water in the palms of his hands, drank his fill. He then washed his face and neck. He unwrapped the kerchief from his arm. It was stuck on the cut and when he pulled it loose, fresh blood began to flow. That was okay as it was better to bleed some, cleaning the wound. He walked to Yancey's horse and scrounging through his saddlebags found some coffee, biscuits, and bacon. "A regular feast," he said smiling. "This is what I need though," he said pulling a bottle of rotgut from the other bag. The whiskey poured on the wounds will help keep the infection down and drinking enough of it will help with the pain. He also found a clean shirt that he quickly tore into strips to use as a bandage.

He sat back down and inspected the wound. The blood was now just a small trickle. "Might as well as get this over with," he said pouring some of the contents of the bottle on the cut. He face contorted in pain as the whiskey burned his arm something fierce.

"DAMN!!" he cursed loudly. He stood up jumping around for a few seconds till the pain subsided some. He wrapped the wound with a clean bandage from Yancey's shirt and sat down beside the man. The man's face was almost unrecognizable. His left eye was closed due to the swelling of his cheek that was crushed. His nose was busted from Tye's knee but otherwise, was okay unless maybe a rib or two was broke. Secretly, Tye hoped they were. "The more you suffer the happier I'm gonna be," he said as he poured a small amount from the bottle on Yancey's cut wrist. He smiled when the unconscious man groaned but didn't wake up.

He piled some rocks in a small circle and built a very small fire. The rocks were about a foot high and would hide the flames. He collected some water from the creek in the coffee pot and put it on the rocks to boil. He placed a skillet on the fire and put the bacon in to fry. He sat back and relaxed, his stomach growling louder as the aroma of the bacon reached his nostrils. In a couple of minutes, he was eating bacon and biscuits that had been soaked in the hot bacon grease; a real feast to a hungry man. The coffee topped everything off. He checked the sun again and figured he only had thirty minutes of good light left. He decided to camp here. He had retrieved Sandy and both horses had plenty of grass and water. He put some more rocks around the fire and made it a little larger. It was probably going to get in the forties tonight and with him hurt and Yancey hurting, they would be subject of catching pneumonia. He pulled Yancey closer to the fire and checked the rope on his hands and feet. Satisfied, he laid a blanket on the outlaw. He pulled his bedroll out and slipped under the blanket. He was warm and snug, and it did not take long for his exhausted body to relax. The last thing he remembered seeing was the setting sun.

~~~

Buff knew they were running out of time. It would be suicide to stay in these rocks after dark. No way could these men handle Apaches in the dark. By staying, they would be there permanently by morning. They were half through the jumbled rocks now and it had been thirty minutes since Reynolds was killed. Suddenly, two shots rang out almost in unison. An Apache that Absher shot fell from atop the rock that Buff was circling and almost fell on top of him. The Apache hit the ground hard but was up and charged Buff with his knife, one arm hanging limp where Absher's bullet had struck him. He drove the knife deep into Buff's left shoulder and both men fell, rolling on the ground. Buff pulled his knife and drove it into the Apache's belly, ripping it upwards. The Apache's black eyes were afire with hate, but the fire in them quickly dimmed... and he died.

Phipps wasn't so lucky. The Apache Christian shot released an arrow just as he was hit that caught Phipps high in the right side of his chest, just under the shoulder. The arrow protruded about six inches from his back as Phipps sat down, holding the feathered shaft with his left hand. He was in a state of shock so the pain had not set in yet.

Paddock ordered Christian and Absher to get Phipps and Buff and fall back, out of the rocks. The lieutenant and Roberts covered them as they retrieved the wounded men.

Paddock, after the wounded men were safely out and lying on the ground, said "We are going back in and get Reynolds. I don't want them bastards mutilating him. Let's go." They were back where Buff and Phipps were in about five minutes with Reynolds body.

Paddock ordered. "Move Buff and Phipps into the mesquite stand that we were in earlier. Then one of you get Reynolds's body in here and the other get Jones and the horses in here quick." 'Damn', Paddock thought to himself. 'One dead, two wounded, and four dead Apaches. That leaves two or three of them and three of us that are able to fight. I figure they will try and get one or two more of us tonight...maybe all of us.' "Sonofabitch," he mumbled.

Absher said. "Sir?'

Paddock not realizing he had been thinking out loud said. "No fire tonight, men. The horses are good sentries but I want two of us awake at all times. I figure they may try to sneak in and finish us off in the dark. Let's look at the wounds before it's completely dark."

Buff said in a whispered voice. "Git me klose ta Phipps." They moved him carefully beside the moaning man. "This is whut yu do. Lootenant. Take my Bowie an kut tha shaft whare it kumes out his back." Roberts did this. "Gud," Buff said. He was woozy, sweat rolling down his face. "Wun uf yu git behind him and hold him tite Wun uf yu grab that thar shaft in front and kount to three outloud. On three, yu jerk that shaft hard and get if out.

Phipps screamed as the shaft came out. Buff said. "Pore sum uf that whesky in tha holes, frunt and back and then bandage it up." Buff groaned and passed out. Paddock pulled Buff's shirt off and looked at the nasty looking purple cut where the knife went in. He almost threw up but managed to hold the bile in his belly down.

Paddock said to Roberts and Christian. "That is one tough sonofabitch...and a damn good man telling us how to take care of

161

Phipps there before himself." He cleaned around the purple slit in Buff's shoulder. He poured whiskey in it and Buff groaned but stayed unconscious. They put his shirt back on him and lay him and Phipps in their bedrolls.

Paddock said. "Private Jones, you and Christian take the first watch. You doze off and your hair will be on an Apaches' lance by morning. Absher and I will relieve you about midnight. Stay awake and alert or we are all dead. Understood?"

Both men nodded and said "Yes Sir." The horses were only a few feet away and were securely picketed and for extra protection, hobbled also. To make sure the men stayed awake; they sit side by side, facing opposite detections. This way, if one dozed the other would see it. It was now full dark and the camp was set.

Jones and Christian's watch passed painfully slow and both men's nerves were on edge. An owl screeched as it flew over the camp and Jones jumped as if he had been shot. Christian whispered.

"We have to relax, Jones. If that had been Apaches, You would have missed and might have shot yourself...or me. Take a deep breath, exhale slowly and relax. I'm right beside you." Things were quite the rest of their watch. They were relieved at midnight by Absher and Paddock.

Paddock asked Christian. "Everything quiet?"

"Yes Sir."

"You and Jones get about three hours sleep, then relieve us."

"Will do, Sir." The lieutenant and Absher sat where Christian and Jones had been sitting. It was so dark that you had to depend more on your hearing than your eyes. The horses were quiet and the only sound that the men could hear was the horses munching the short grama grass. Both men were so up tight that neither had any problem staying awake. Christian and Jones had a little trouble relaxing and falling asleep but finally, the light snoring of both men reached Paddock's ears. He smiled, glad they could relax. They needed the rest after the events of the last twenty-four hours.

Buff stirred, and sat up, groaning with the pain in his left shoulder. He blinked his eyes trying to figure out where he was. The pain in his shoulder reminded him.

"Whut time is it, Looteenant?" he whispered.

"About three a.m." He reached over and lightly shook Christian awake. "Time," Paddock whispered. Christian woke up Jones who mumbled something no one understood...and probably didn't want to.

Paddock asked. "How's the shoulder?"

"Wale, I kno it's thar," Buff replied. "Phipps still out?"

"Yes. Probably best for him. His breathing is okay so I don't think the arrow got his lungs."

"That's gud. Listen, Lootenant. If'n I kno Injuns, tha will kome in abut an hour befo full lite. Don't thank anee uf us had better go ta sleep. When tha kome, it will be quick so we got ta be reddy. Be karful cause it's gonna be klose in fiting so be shur it's an Injun yur shuting at." Christian and Jones heard this warning but didn't need it to stay awake...Jones could swear the men at Fort Clark could hear his heart beating. Christian had been in several fights with the Apache and never had been scared...till now. There was just something damn scary about waiting...waiting to have a stinking Apache try and cave your skull in. Paddock and Absher lay on their bedrolls with their pistols in their hands acting as if they were asleep. Buff lay with his pistol in his hand, his Bowie on his stomach.

～～～

Nasay saw the men change positions. He was preparing to attack with his two men but decided to wait. He knew soldiers and knew they would be most vulnerable after they had been on watch for an hour or so. Right now they were alert for anything.

Two hours passed and Nasay signaled the other two. One moved to the left of Nasay and the other to the right. Even though they were in thick mesquite, they moved as quite as ghosts. They would attack quickly and silently with knives and tomahawks from three directions at once. It was time and Nasay braced himself for the attack.

Gary McMillan

Chapter Twenty

"AIEEE!!" The blood curdling shriek that came from Nasay's and the other two Apaches' throats so close to where the soldiers were sitting had the desired affect Nasay wanted. Private Jones, startled, accidentally discharged his pistol, the bullet almost hitting his own outstretched foot. Nasay was on him before he could cock the Navy Colt again. He screamed as Nasay's knife slicded deep into his chest. He grabbed Nasay's hand with both of his but could not prevent the warrior from jerking the knife out and plunging it again deep into his chest. He screamed "moma" and then choked as bright red froth bubbled out of his mouth. Nasay held him up and swung again with the knife and catching the man's throat, almost severed the head.

Christian was startled also but managed to get a quick shot at the Apache warrior who was only three strides from him when he came out of the brush. His bullet struck the warrior in the left shoulder. The force of the bullet at this close range knocked him backwards. He recovered quickly however, and charged again. Christian aimed and as he was pulling the trigger, his wrist was smashed by an unknown object, the gun falling from his numb fingers. Nasay had struck his arm with his club and drew back to deliver the killing blow to Christian's head when something hit him in the side, knocking the wind out of him. He stepped back, the realization of what happened not registering yet.

He fell to the ground trying to suck in air. His mouth filled with dirt, choking him, as he lay on the ground trying to get air into his lungs. Then, a burning pain like he had never felt before coursed through his body. He tried to raise himself up but fell back on his back. The last thing he saw was the sun peeking over the hills.

Buff lay back, his pistol smoking, knowing that was one of the luckiest shots he had ever made. He was so weak that he had not been able to hold the gun steady. The third Apache charged past him, straight at the back of Lieutenant Paddock. Buff yelled at the lieutenant but he knew it was too late. He had cocked the Colt again as soon as he had fired at the other Apache. He shifted the gun to the right a little and aimed at the warrior's back. It took all his strength to pull the trigger just as the knife started its downward plunge, intended for Paddock's back. The bullet struck the brave right between the shoulder blades and exploded out his chest. Paddock's back was covered in the Apache's blood.

The Indian Christian had wounded was back in the fight, swinging his club at Christian's head. Christian fell backwards, the club barely clipping him on the forehead. A shot rang out and the Apache stiffened, stood up straight and looked at the hole in his chest. He dropped the club and slowly crumpled to the ground. Christian looked to his right and saw Absher holding a revolver, his eyes as big as saucers.

The furious fight was over in less than six seconds. The suddenness and the ferocity of the attack shocked everyone except Buff. As the realization set in that it was over, Paddock and Absher stood up, looking around at the carnage. Blood was everywhere including all over Paddock's uniform. The three warriors lay where they had fallen. Paddock lost what little food he had on his stomach when he saw Jones sitting with his back to them, his head hanging back, dead eyes starring at Paddock.

Christian was bent over, holding his broken wrist. Phipps was still out and Buff was almost unconscious. Paddock fixed Christian's wrist the best they could, making a makeshift splint from mesquite limbs. Absher took care of Jones's body, wrapping it in a bloody blanket.

Paddock sat down beside Christian. He nodded toward Buff who was now unconscious.

He said. "I guess you know we owe both our lives to that old man over there."

"Yes Sir. I won't forget it either when he wakes up. He's something else, Sir. I would have liked to seen him forty years ago in those mountains. I bet he was something else."

"Hell, Christian, he's something else now." They both smiled. Absher came and sat down with them.

"You did great, Private," Paddock said, patting him on the shoulder.

"I was scared, Sir. Scared to death," Absher whispered.

"Scared or not, you did what you had to do. If you and Buff had not killed those Apaches, all our scalps would be hanging on lances now," Paddock said. "Hell, you wasn't any more scared than me. I couldn't even spit." He stood up and spoke to Absher. "Let's get things together and check on Buff and Phipps." They removed the dead Apache warriors, started a fire, and put on some coffee.

Phipps started to moan some so they moved to take a look at him. His eyes were still closed but he was in some pain. "He's gonna be really hurting when he comes around," Absher stated.

Paddock answered. "I know he is. We have less than a bottle of whiskey left. That's not enough to dull the pain for all three."

"Jus give it ta them," Buff said, his voice startling both men. "I've been hurt wurse than this befo...I'll make it." He lay back down and shut his eyes. Truth was he was in considerable pain. 'I'll be dammed if'n I sho how much it hurts ta these here soldur boys. Been braggin too long as ta how tuft us old monton men wure.' He wished now he had never opened his mouth about that.

Paddock looked at all three men's wounds and it appeared none were festering. We'll get a bite to eat, drink some coffee, and then head toward the fort.

Buff asked. "Yu boys kno how ta make a travois to carry Phipps?"

"No," Paddock answered. "But you can tell us." Buff explained to them how to build it and how to tie the poles to the horse. It only took a few minutes and by the time they finished the aroma of fresh coffee filtered through the camp. Phipps was starting to regain full consciousness and beginning to be aware of the pain he was going to have shortly. Absher placed his hand under Phipps head, raising

167

him up enough to pour some of the whiskey down him. He coughed a little and some of the liquid ran down his chin. Absher made him drink almost half of the bottle. He lost consciousness again and Paddock and Absher carefully laid him on the travois.

Paddock said. "We'll drink some coffee real quick, break camp and be on our way." He nodded toward Phipps. "That man needs some medical attention quick."

Buff, his back against a boulder asked. "Does aneewun kno whare tha thar creek we crossed last evening komes frum?"

Christian sitting next to Buff holding his bandaged wrist against his stomach replied. "I wouldn't swear to it but I believe that may be Los Moras that heads up at the fort."

"Be my guess too." Buff said. "Whut do yu thank, Lootenant?"

"It's clear with a good volume of water coming down it. Could be Los Moras."

"We kud follur it fur a while and see." Buff said.

"Break camp," Paddock ordered. Absher tightened the girths on the saddles and helped Buff and Christian in the saddle. Jones, wrapped in his blanket lay across the saddle and was securely tied to it. Buff almost passed out from the pain when he first stood up. Once settled into the saddle the discomfort eased some…until his horse took the first step. It felt like a hot poker was in his shoulder. "This heer is going ta be a long, long damn day," he said, cursing under his breath.

Christian had made a sling from his bandana and his right arm rested in it. His fingers were swollen and slightly blue in color. His arm ached considerably, but it could have been a hell of lot worse. He would be dead if Absher had not killed the Apache. He felt of his forehead. There was a small cut crusted over in blood from the club had nicked him.

Paddock, in the lead looked back over his shoulder at what was left of his patrol. 'We are a sorry looking lot,' he thought, 'but every damn man is a man…a soldier. He was proud of them. He thought it had been a successful patrol despite the losses and injuries. He hoped major Thurston did too.

Buff pulled his horse up besides Paddock's mount. "Kongratulations, Lootenant."

Paddock looked at Buff and asked. "Congratulations! What for?"

"Dun got yourself bloodied. Yu handled yourself reel wale for a greener. Tha word will get round tha fort tha yu are okay to ride tha river with." Buff smiled, despite the pain in the shoulder. "A lot uf officers have ta go on a lot uf patrols before tha git tested like yu did on yur ferst wun. Yur gonna be alright, Lootenant."

Paddock wasn't sure exactly the meaning of all that Buff said but he figured it was a compliment and he felt good about things. He knew one thing for sure. That old man was one tough sonofabitch. They found the creek and headed north.

~~~

Tye struggled out of his bedroll just before first light. He thought he heard what sounded like gunshots coming in on the southerly breeze but had listened for a few seconds more and heard nothing. He thought he was just hearing things. He had slept a lot later than he normally does but damn, he was just totally drained of energy. Yancey was conscious and moaning and groaning like some little kid. He figured that was what had woke him up. He struggled to his feet and walked to where Yancey was lying.

Tye asked. "Hurting some, Yance?"

"Go to hell, Watkins." He said grimacing. "How come you didn't just kill me?"

Tye hesitated a moment before answering. "Probably should have and I might yet. The temptation is there, I promise you."

Yancey groaned. "I gotta pee."

"Go ahead."

"I can't pee in my pants you crazy bastard," Yancey screamed.

Tye mused over the situation for a moment. "Tell you what Yancey. I'll untie you but if you try to run, I won't kill you, I'll shoot you in both legs. That should add to your suffering some." He moved over and untied the man's legs and then his hands, holding the gun on him all the time. Tye backed off. "Get your business done…and be quick about it."

Yancey stood up slowly, swaying back and forth barely keeping his balance. He turned his back on Tye and slowly walked a few steps and relieved his bladder. He thought about trying to make a break for it and get a quick killing bullet but he knew Tye would do what he said he would. He was suffering enough now, he didn't need more. He stumbled back to Tye and held out his hands. Tye tied them and told him to sit over there, nodding to a place by the fire. Yancey obeyed and sat down.

Tye rekindled the fire and put some coffee on to boil. He pitched Yancey a piece of jerky before getting a piece for himself. He sat down and chewed the jerky, watching Yancey. He had never hated a man before nor had he actually wanted to kill a man as bad as he did this piece of shit. He decided if the outlaw said one more thing to him, he would shoot him in both kneecaps and then he might just do something else to give him some real pain. God he hated that man.

Yancey noticed Tye staring at him. He could tell from Tye's expression that it would not be wise to say anything or complain about his arm or busted cheek or anything else. They just sat there in silence, chewing their jerky, Tye wanting Yancey to give him an excuse and Yancey wishing he had high-tailed it out of the country after the escape from jail.

Sandy nickered and twitched his ears. Tye was up in a flash and behind a boulder wondering what Sandy had heard…or seen. Then he heard it…the unmistakable sound of horses, camp equipment clanging, and saddles squeaking. He stood up as the patrol, or what was left of it, came into camp. Tye immediately saw Buff and ran to him.

"BUFF," he yelled. "What in hell are you doing out here?" he asked angrily. "You were supposed to be watching Rebecca."

"I…I kno tha, Tye," he mumbled. "Majur tol me…" he passed out and fell off his horse. Tye caught him and set him gently on the ground.

Paddock said. "Due to circumstances, Major Thurston asked him to scout for us. We lost your tracks the morning after the snow. I sent a dispatch to Thurston explaining we had lost your tracks and asking what I should do. He asked Buff if he would help us find you. He promised Buff he would take care of Rebecca and he moved her to the O'Malley's and doubled the guard. That old man went right to work and found where you camped and your tracks away from camp. He kept us on them till we crossed the Apache tracks. He followed them and in a couple fights, we killed all of them. It wasn't cheap as you can see," nodding toward what was left of his men. Is that Yancey over there?"

Tye nodded and sat down on the ground cradling Buff's head in his lap. He looked under the bandage and saw the nasty cut. "He's gonna be okay," Tye said, "If we can get him to the fort and the doctor."

"He going to be fine, Tye. That is the toughest sonofabitch..." then caught himself. "I mean he's the toughest old man I ever saw. He was laid up with that wound when the Apaches that were left attacked us. He killed two of the three including one that was fixing to knife me in the back. I," he paused. "No, all of us owe him a lot. I grew up back east reading the novels about him and the other mountain men He's everything I ever thought that a mountain man would be. He earned all of our respect and I expect everyone at the fort when they hear about it."

Tye wiped the perspiration off Buff's forehead. "Got any whiskey, Lieutenant?'

Paddock answered. "Just a swallow or so. We have been keeping Phipps drunk to help him with the pain."

"A swallow will do the trick," Tye replied.

"I'll get the bottle," Christian said. When he returned he handed the bottle to Tye. Tye pressed the bottle to Buff's lips and forced a little down his throat. Buff gagged and his eyes opened, fluttered a couple of times then focused on Tye.

"About Rebecca, I..." he was cut off by Tye.

"I know what happened and I know what you did for Paddock and the others. I'm proud of you, Buff...very proud." He pulled

Buff's head to his chest and hugged him for a minute. Buff's good arm went around Tye's waist. Tye looked up at Paddock.

"We need to get the wounded to the fort, Sir." He helped Buff on his horse and then walked over to Yancey. He reached down and grabbed his wrist, jerking him to his feet.

"Get your ass on that horse and be quick about it."

"I ain't moving." Yancey answered.

Tye walked to Yancey's horse and removed the rope that was around the pommel. "You'll get on that horse," he said as he dropped the loop around Yancey's wrist and jerked it tight, "or I'll drag your ass back to the fort; makes me no difference either way."

"You would to, wouldn't you?" Yancey said getting to his feet. When everyone was mounted they headed north, toward the fort which was almost a full days ride away.

Chapter Twenty-One

The patrol did not stop for several hours. Not a word was said by anyone except Yancey. He was continually bitching about the treatment he was receiving. At one point Absher threatened him.

He said. "Yancey, for the bad-ass you are supposed to be you have got to be the biggest damn baby I have ever saw. You don't hear Buff complaining or Phipps either, and they are both hurt worse than you. If you are an example of what was supposed to be the tough Confederate soldiers," he paused. "It's no wonder ya'll lost the war."

"GO TO HELL YOU YANKEE BASTARD!" Yancey yelled. Absher turned in the saddle and looked back at Yancey who was trailing right behind him.

He said angrily. "If you say one more word...if you make one more sound, Yancey, I'm gonna slap you so hard on that busted cheek of yours that you will be hurting so bad you will be praying to get that rope around your neck to get you out of your misery. Course then," he said with a wicked smile, "Your other misery will begin...in hell." Yancey became quiet as a Church mouse. Tye smiled and Buff, riding beside Absher, reached with his good arm and patted him on the shoulder.

After a few more minutes, Tye suggested they stop and rest the horses. He also suggested that Paddock send a man ahead to tell Thurston they were coming in with Yancey. Paddock sent Absher since he was the only man not wounded besides himself. Tye told him. "Keep riding due north, do not follow the creek which meanders in every direction and increasing the distance. It should be about four miles to the Old Mail Road and when you reach it,

173

turn west and get to the fort. Ask major Thurston to send an ambulance and surgeon east. We will meet them on the Old Mail Road. Also tell them about the wounded men at the Bradley place." Tye knew where the homestead was and he drew a map so whomever Thurston sent could find it.

Absher had left and after about twenty minutes, Tye and Paddock helped everyone very carefully back in the saddle...except Yancey. Tye did not tighten the girth on Yancey's saddle, accidentally, and when Yancey toed the stirrup and put his weight on it, the saddle slipped sideways. Yancey hit the ground hard, jarring every bone in his body especially his busted cheek bone. He came up cursing loudly.

Tye apologized. "Sorry about that Yancey, my mistake." He mounted Sandy and looking straight ahead, smiled. Lieutenant Paddock behind him smiled as did Christian who was behind Yancey and leading the horse that pulled the travois that Phipps lay on. Phipps, awake now, knew what had happened and despite the pain he was enduring, had to laugh.

Phipps mumbled, "What he's going thru now ain't nothing compared to what's coming to him in the hereafter."

They reached the Old Mail Road about an hour before dusk. They had not traveled a quarter of a mile when Tye saw the Ambulance and an escort of soldiers coming toward them. He turned back to Paddock who was half asleep in the saddle.

"Ambulance is coming, Sir."

Paddock jerked his head up and looked. He saw the wagon coming with the escort and turning in the saddle he told Christian to sit tall in the saddle and close up ranks. He dusted his uniform off the best he could and beat the dust off of his hat on his leg. He sat as straight as an arrow in the saddle.

A minute later, much to his surprise, Thurston arrived ahead of the ambulance. The major rode up beside him.

Paddock saluted. "Good to see you Sir." He saw Thurston looking past him. "The prisoner...Yancey Cates, Sir."

"He looks a little beat up," Lieutenant, Thurston said in a stern voice.

"Yes Sir. We've had a hard time keeping him on his horse. Seems he keeps falling off and hurting himself."

"I see." The major said smiling. "Accidents do happen. I want your full report on everything that happened when we arrive back to the fort and you have had time to rest some." He turned and looked at the arriving ambulance and the rest of the escort. He turned back to Paddock, "Lieutenant, for your first patrol you did well. As a matter fact, despite the losses, you did an exceptional job. Congratulations." He reached out and shook Paddock's hand.

"Thank you, Sir."

The ambulance pulled up and the door flew open and Tye could not believe what he saw. Rebecca, tears streaming down her face ran toward him. He reached down from the saddle with his good arm and lifted her by the waist up to him.

"I love you, Tye. I love you," she said, as her warm lips met his. Whistles and yells came from the escort but a look from Tye shut them up immediately. He kissed Rebecca again before putting her on Sandy behind him. He then tipped his hat to the men and smiled.

Thurston came over to him. "Outstanding job Tye; to be honest with you I figured you would bring Yancey in across the saddle."

"Thought about it Major. I thought about it a lot. You are no more surprised than I am. I just couldn't do it. I could not kill a man in cold blood, not even a man I hated as much as Yancey."

The men in the escort placed Phipps in the ambulance as well as Christian. The doctor was checking both men's injuries. He had already looked at Buff's and thought he would be okay but would be bedridden for a few days. Tye reined Sandy back to where Buff sat on his horse. Rebecca leaned over and kissed him on the cheek and gave him a hug.

Buff whispered, "Everthang is okay Rebecca. Tye, I hope yu ar reedy fur sum more of thos stories abut yur pa."

"I can't wait, Buff," he said patting him on the shoulder. "Let's all go home."

~~~

The next -day, at noon, without a lot of notice, Yancey met his maker on the gallows. He did himself proud though. He walked up the steps, never said a word and refused the hood over his head. He was looking straight at Tye when the trap door opened. Several men watched Yancey die... a lot of satisfied men.

Thurston was a satisfied man. He had a new Lieutenant he could count on along with Lieutenant Garrison. He had Captain McClellan whom he could trust. He had one of the best sergeants in the army in Master Sergeant O'Malley, he had the best damn scout in the whole United States Army, and he might just have the second best in Buff. What more could he ask for. He lit up his cigar and headed back to his office.

Gary McMillan

Gary McMillan